Butterfly Heart

Also by Moa Backe Åstot

Fire from the Sky

Butterfly

Moa Backe Åstot

Translated by AGNES BROOMÉ

Heart

LQ
LEVINE QUERIDO

Montclair | Amsterdam | Hoboken

This is an Em Querido book
Published by Levine Querido

LQ
LEVINE QUERIDO

www.levinequerido.com • info@levinequerido.com

Levine Querido is distributed by Chronicle Books, LLC

Copyright © 2023 by Moa Backe Åstot
English translation copyright © 2025 by Agnes Broomé

Originally published in Sweden in 2023 as *Fjärilshjärta* by Rabén & Sjögren
Published by agreement with Salomonsson Agency

All rights reserved

Library of Congress Control Number: 2024950964
ISBN 978-1-64614-575-1
Printed and bound in China

Published October 2025

First Printing

Butterfly Heart

1

THE GÁBDDE'S TOO small for Vilda. It's Mom's old one, the one she wore to her confirmation—a dark blue, knee-length Jokkmokk gábdde with red, yellow, and green detailing. Mom must have been a really small fifteen-year-old, because Vilda's arms are too long and her stomach's too big, even though she's not even fourteen.

"Bah," Mom exclaims, picking up a newspaper and fanning her shiny forehead. "We need someone who knows how to sew. At times like these, I really regret not asking my mom to teach me while she was still alive."

Vilda has never had her own gábdde. Her little sister, Irma, hasn't, either. And Áhkko died so long ago, Vilda doesn't really have any memories of her. She knows her only from photographs and home videos. And through Áddjá's memories, of course. He often talks about Áhkko as though she were still with them. Áddjá has a lot of skills, but sewing is definitely not one of them.

Mom tugs on the gábdde one last time, but it still doesn't fit. Vilda feels like a balloon inside it, as though the fabric might rip at any moment. But even so, she twirls in front of the mirror, imagining what she would look like if the gábdde *had* fit. She might even have looked beautiful.

"Oh, well, we'll cross that bridge when we get to it," Mom says. "After all, there's no rush. As far as I know, we have no weddings or funerals coming up this summer."

What Mom doesn't understand is that there absolutely *is* a rush. At least that's how it feels to Vilda. She has never wanted a gábdde more than she does right now. No one at school believes her when she tells them she's Sámi. No one except Alma, but she has always known. Their other classmates ask a thousand questions and are never satisfied with her answers. Do you speak Sámi? Just a little. Do you have any reindeer? No, Vilda doesn't, but her grandpa does. Is your dad Sámi? No, but her mom is. Oh, right, they say at that, as though everything's suddenly clear. So you're only *half* Sámi. *Only*, as though that's not Sámi enough.

The students who had attended Sámi school until sixth grade came to Vilda's school for seventh grade. Seeing them in their gábde at the last day of school ceremony really brought home what she was missing.

She hopes things will be different after the summer, when they start eighth grade. Then everyone will accept that she really is Sámi. They won't be able to question it if she has her own gábdde.

Mom strokes Vilda's shoulder. "Áddjá's going to be so proud when he sees you in a gábdde for the first time. His little butterfly."

Vilda tries to imagine her grandpa's reaction: his eyes lighting up—maybe he'll even clap. She feels warm just thinking about it. Her darling, darling áddjá.

"Can I go see him?"

"Of course you can, if he has time before we're off to Sundsvall."

"And can I check if any of Áhkko's gábde fit me?"

"You'll have to talk to your áddjá about that. They're all at his house, after all."

Vilda needs Mom's help to get out of the gábdde. It's stuck, refusing to let go. When it finally comes off, Vilda collapses onto her bed and lies there in her bra and underpants. Mom fans her with the newspaper, opening the window with her other hand. A breeze finds its way into the room, giving Vilda's sweaty skin goose bumps.

She closes her eyes and listens to the birds singing in the trees outside, a bumblebee buzzing near the open window. Feeling a thousand possibilities swirling up inside her.

2

THE WIND CARRIES with it the sweet fragrance of lilacs. Vilda's hair is wet and tangled—there's no point trying to run her fingers through it. They're just going to get stuck. The baby hair by her ear flutters in the breeze; it always dries faster than the rest. She'd like to cut off every last fine, downy hair. It looks ridiculous.

"It's kind of funny that you of all people are named Vilda," Alma says. "Don't you think?"

"Why?"

"Since you're not exactly *wild*."

Vilda shifts in her lounge chair, and her weight makes the legs rise up on one side, nearly tipping it. Alma sprawls in the lounger next to hers, face turned to the sun, eyes closed. The skin along her hairline is pale.

"Well, my parents didn't know that when I was born."

"I suppose. It's just funny to think about."

Alma's bikini top is hot pink. White skin peeks out through the gaps in it. Vilda's still wearing her old bikini with the strawberry print. Her nipples are showing through the fabric. She hates it, but

Mom won't let her buy a new one yet. *We only just bought this one*, Mom keeps saying. How can she not see that it's too small? *Hello*, Vilda's not twelve anymore.

Alma squints at Vilda. "I texted Casper yesterday."

"Seriously?" The lounger creaks beneath Vilda. "What did *you* say? And what did *he* say?"

"I just asked what he was doing. He read it but didn't reply, so after a while, I wrote again, but that message wasn't even delivered. Maybe he has no reception."

"Maybe he read the first one and was so happy to hear from you he dropped his phone in the toilet. And then he couldn't reply, and never saw the second message."

Alma rolls her eyes. "All right, come on, now you have to tell me who you're in love with!"

"No one," Vilda replies. As usual.

"Fine, but seriously, though. Don't you at least have a crush on someone?"

She shakes her head. It's the truth. She doesn't have a crush on anyone and Alma knows it. Who would she even be in love with anyway? Not one of the guys in their class, that's for sure. Alma found Casper on a ski slope during Easter break. He's about to start upper secondary and looks like a film star—long, wavy hair and sparkling eyes. None of the guys in their class looks like that. Several of them are shorter than the girls, and they're always wearing sweatpants and spending their nights playing video games.

"So, are you excited to go on holiday tomorrow?"

"Don't try to change the subject! But yes. And I figure I'm going to meet loads of fit guys in Cyprus." Alma smiles, her eyes still closed. "Good luck finding one *here*! Actually, you should pick someone up in Sundsvall when you go."

Vilda snorts derisively. She doesn't want to think about having to spend two straight weeks with Mom, Dad, and Irma. Not to mention Dad's extended family. Maybe she should move in with Áddjá and let the rest of the family go to Sundsvall without her. And then she could just stay with him for the rest of the summer, until school starts back up. Sometimes, it feels like Áddjá's the only person who never gets annoyed with her. Who likes her just the way she is.

"Seriously, though, I'm going to be away for three weeks. Three! You won't even recognize me when I come back."

"And you won't recognize me after I've been force-fed biscuits by my grandparents every day for two weeks," Vilda says.

Alma giggles. It makes her dimples pop out.

How is Vilda supposed to get by without her for three weeks? There are so many things she's going to miss. Their inside jokes. The way Alma squeals and cries when she laughs. The way she talks in her sleep when they stay over at each other's houses. Not even then is she quiet. Her voice has always been loud and clear, as though she always knows exactly what she wants to say. She's never been afraid to make herself heard, unlike Vilda. Even so, they've always been best friends.

"What else are you going to do while I'm gone?"

"Miss you, I guess."

"Aww. Aren't you going to hang with Erica and them?"

"I guess. After we get back. But before we go to Sundsvall, I'm going to Áddjá's to see if he has a gábdde that fits me."

This time Alma's the one who turns over in her lounger. So she faces Vilda, looking a little mischievous, as though an exciting thought has just occurred to her.

"Guys in gábde—aren't they just criminally good-looking?"

Vilda groans. And yet, there's a sudden spark of something inside her. "Just stop!"

"Don't you think you'll want to get with a Sámi guy, though?"

"How am I supposed to know that now?"

"Well, you're Sámi," Alma says, shrugging. "So it would make sense if you wanted to be with someone who's Sámi, too."

"Except you're not Sámi, and we're practically a couple."

"In your dreams!"

Alma sticks her tongue out at Vilda. Vilda sticks her tongue out, too, leaning forward to touch Alma's face with it. Their chairs almost tip over when Alma, laughing hysterically, tries to push Vilda away.

One of Alma's hands is still pressing against Vilda when she picks up her phone. The screen looks black, even though it's lit. She squints as she reads. Vilda can't see anything.

"I guess he managed to fish his phone out of the toilet and dried it off with a hair dryer or whatever, because he's read everything now."

"And he didn't reply?"

"Nope. But we don't need Casper anyway."

Alma sits up, tossing her hair back over her shoulder. Then she jumps up and does a wobbly dance on the lawn.

Vilda gets up, too. The grass is warm under her bare feet. They sing. Alma sounds insane and leads Vilda in a lindy hop. Vilda's stomach muscles ache, and Alma's moving so fast she trips. They stop, panting.

"Honestly, I feel sorry for him," Alma whispers, her forehead against Vilda's. It's hot and sweaty. "He doesn't know what he's missing, dissing two cool girls like us."

3

MOM'S CUTTING VEGETABLES. Irma stands next to her, gnawing the end of a cucumber. Vilda's at the kitchen table, stirring her chocolate milk so furiously the glass tinkles, her eyes on Mom and Irma, the pale green mush in her sister's mouth. The two bright-red mosquito bites on Irma's forehead.

Mom turns around. "Vilda, sweetheart, have you started packing?"

"Huh?"

"We're leaving for Sundsvall in just a few days, you know. I can write you a packing list, if you want, unless you've already made one?"

Vilda drops her cheese on toast on her napkin. "But I have to go see Áddjá before we go!"

"Why?"

"You know why! To try on Áhkko's gábde!"

Mom tilts the cutting board, sweeping the cucumber pieces into a bowl.

"Calm down, angel. Why don't you ride your bike over there today, then? It's almost lunch, but I can't imagine you're very hungry, given as how you're only just having breakfast."

Vilda takes a bite of her toast. "Why can't you drive me?"

"I'm making lunch, and a bit of exercise won't hurt you."

Vilda drinks the last of her chocolate milk, leaving the spoon in her glass. Doesn't clean up after herself, because Mom and Irma are blocking the kitchen counter.

Dad's mowing the lawn. Vilda breathes in the smell. Few things smell more like summer vacation than freshly cut grass.

She runs over to him, waving her arms. "Can you give me a ride to Áddjá's house?"

"Right now?" Dad rubs his forehead. It's red. "I thought we were about to have lunch?"

"Mom said I could go."

"Right?"

"But she can't drive me because she's cooking," Vilda adds. "So I figured I'd ask you."

He looks skeptical. But then he pulls the car key out of his pocket. "Get in. I'll be there in a second."

ÁDDJÁ OPENS THE door before Vilda can knock. She falls into his arms, letting him stroke her back with his big hand. Burrows her nose into his T-shirt, breathing in his smell. Fresh summer breeze, morning coffee, and forest. And something else, too, something warm and familiar. Granddad smell.

"My darling butterfly," he says.

She stays there with her head against his chest, listening to the sounds his body makes. His heart beating, his stomach gurgling.

The stairs creak as they climb them. When Áddjá opens the door to the walk-in closet in the bedroom, they're greeted by a stuffy smell. The closet's like a little den. A few shelves along the walls hold hats, boxes, and shoes. Gábde on hangers, lined up on a long rod. Vilda touches one of the sleeves, fingering the cuff. It's circled by three stripes—blue, yellow, and red.

"So," Áddjá says. "Which one would you like to try on?"

"All of them!"

Gábdde after gábdde ends up on the bedspread. Áhkko owned a lot of gábde, most in shades of blue or black. Vilda's looking for a belt on the top shelf when Áddjá stops her.

"Not that shelf," he says. "There's nothing fun up there."

Instead, he pulls out a brown box from the shelf underneath. Brushes the dust off the lid.

"If you're going to wear a gábdde, you need a sliehppá, too."

In the box is a red, traditional dickey. The collar is decorated with pewter thread embroidery and the bib with a small embroidered cross.

"Do you think it'll fit me?" Vilda asks.

It does. Áddjá pushes Vilda's hair out of the way, buttons up the sliehppá, and ties it around her back. It's just a little big around the collar, but that's okay.

"And then the gábdde goes over it," Áddjá says.

She tries on two gábde from different periods of Áhkko's life before they find one that fits like a glove. The fabric falls nicely around Vilda's body. The weight of it, the steady pressure of the belt around her waist, makes her feel safe. Whole, somehow. As though the gábdde is holding her together.

A shudder runs through her, a whirling light. Her smile stretches and turns into a laugh. She twirls to let Áddjá admire her.

"So what do you think?"

....

He clears his throat. His voice sounds thick. "Tjáppa, fávros niejddam."

Vilda stops midtwirl. Suddenly doesn't know what to do. Even though she understands him, she can't bring herself to say anything back. Áddjá only ever speaks Sámi with their older relatives, never with Vilda or Irma. Or Mom. What little Vilda understands, she has learned through listening.

She remembers Áddjá's stories from when he was growing up. When he attended the Nomad Boarding School and was forced to speak Swedish instead of Sámi. It was hard for him because at home they spoke only Sámi, and one time he forgot to switch to Swedish when they were playing calf-ear marking in the schoolyard. A teacher heard him, and he was punished—forbidden from ever uttering another word of Sámi at school again.

Vilda can barely begin to imagine what it would be like not to be allowed to speak her native language. It would be like being dumped in a foreign country where you didn't understand a word, and having to get by without your parents.

She shakes off the horrible thought and tries to think of something to say instead. But it doesn't matter that she's dying to reply—she doesn't have the words.

Áddjá sits down on the edge of the bed. His glasses flash when he takes them off. "Dån la áhkut muoduk."

His mouth is open, but she doesn't understand why. His hand trembles when he raises it to his face and wipes the corners of his eyes. Is he crying?

"Boade diek." He waves Vilda over. She nestles next to him and puts her arms around him. Her cheek against his shoulder. He strokes her hair, heavily, as though he's trying to flatten it.

Vilda wishes she had something to say. In this moment, there's nothing she wants more, but she can't. It feels as though someone has opened up her head and disconnected her tongue from her brain. She doesn't want to speak Swedish, but she can't speak Sámi.

The silence is in every part of her, a grinding ache and an emptiness at the same time.

Áddjá makes shushing sounds next to Vilda's ear, as though he's comforting her. But really, it's the other way around, Vilda thinks to herself. Áddjá's the one who needs comforting right now.

She closes her eyes against his shoulder. Lets him keep at it.

THE COFFEE MACHINE is grumbling in the kitchen. Sunlight has settled like a runner down the middle of the table, making Áddjá's cup sparkle. Vilda sits, picking up one of his hand-carved knife handles. Runs a finger over the engraved decorations on it.

Áddjá takes a packet of cookies out of the pantry and pours them onto a plate. "Are you drinking coffee yet?"

She pulls a face. "Yuk, no."

"But you're almost fourteen," he says. "That's a good age to start."

"Seriously? You drank coffee when you were fourteen?"

Áddjá pulls out a chair. She can tell he's stiff; he has to hold on to the table to lower himself onto his seat. Both the wood and his joints creak.

"You'd better believe it," he says. "I was practically an adult when I was fourteen."

It seems like he's about to say more, but then he doesn't. Vilda chooses not to ask what he means. Áddjá's like that sometimes. He'll hint at things, but he often doesn't explain them properly.

About what life as a reindeer herder was like in the olden days, and other things, too. Mysterious things. Mom usually calls Áddjá whenever anyone in the family has a nosebleed, and he always makes it stop. When she was younger, Vilda wanted to know how it worked, but Mom just told her some things can't be explained. So Vilda has stopped asking. At least about things like that.

"Is the knife finished?"

He nods. "That's why I left it out. In case you wanted to see it."

Vilda turns the knife over and over. It is astonishingly beautiful, the engraving so detailed and even. A work of art.

"I wanted to ask you if you'd mind making a design for me to use on the next knife," Áddjá says. "Since you're so good with a pen."

Vilda smiles at the tabletop. As though she were better than him. "Sure, I guess."

"De buorre," Áddjá says. Then he holds out his hand to her. "Vatte munji nijbev."

Once again, her mind freezes as the words land. She pushes the knife over to Áddjá.

He picks it up, pulls the knife out of its sheath, and pushes it back in. Repeats that a few times. Vilda knows he's listening to the click; it has to sound right.

"Can you teach me how to do it?" she asks.

He looks up at her. "Mejt?"

"I want to learn how to make knife handles." She nods toward the knife. "But we have to start right now, before Dad forces me to go to Sundsvall."

"Of course I'll teach you," Áddjá says.

Vilda plays with a strand of her hair. Pushing the ends in under her thumbnail. "Maybe you could teach me something else, too."

Áddjá gives her a searching look. She takes a deep breath, bracing herself.

"I want to speak Sámi."

A smile lurks in the corners of his mouth. "De sámástin máj."

Her stomach flips. Is she finally going to learn now? For real? Suddenly, she's not dreading the summer as much. Maybe she can study while they're in Sundsvall, if she brings books and things? She can always talk to Áddjá on the phone, when they're too far apart to meet up. And imagine how impressed Alma will be when she comes back from Cyprus and hears Vilda speaking Sámi.

Vilda's phone vibrates on the table. She sighs when she hears Mom's voice on the other end.

"We'll be by to pick you up in a minute, so get ready."

"Noooo, come on!"

Áddjá looks like he's chuckling to himself.

"I just got here—do you have to pick me up now?!"

"Yes" is all Mom says before she hangs up.

Áddjá sets the knife on the table so he can say goodbye to Vilda. She hugs him hard, never wants to let go. He rubs her head, making her hair tousled and staticky.

"Vuojnnalin ruvva," he says.

And Vilda knows it's true, they will see each other again soon, but she still can't let go of him. It's simply impossible, she wants nothing more than to stay.

"Can I see you one more time before I go? Maybe tomorrow, if you have time."

"Of course I have time."

It's only when Mom steps through the front door that Vilda realizes she's still wearing the gábdde.

"Wow!" Mom exclaims. But then her smile fades. She looks up at Áddjá, who has followed Vilda into the hallway. "Isn't that her wedding gábdde, Dad?"

Vilda turns and looks at him. He nods. What are they talking about? Is it the gábdde Áhkko wore on the day they got married? Is Vilda really allowed to wear it?

"Dad," Mom says. "I don't think Vilda needs to—"

Mom breaks off, doesn't finish her sentence.

"She can borrow it for now." And then Áddjá gets that mischievous look in his eye again, as though he has a secret.

Vilda looks down at her body in the gábdde. To think that Áhkko wore it at her actual wedding. Vilda has seen photographs of Áhkko and Áddjá on their wedding day, black-and-white ones. Áhkko wore a tiara. Both she and Áddjá were so beautiful, like a prince and princess. When Vilda gets married, she wants to be just as beautiful. Both she and the guy will be wearing gábde, just like Alma said, and Vilda will have a tiara in her hair, too, with a veil to go with it.

"You're pretty as a butterfly in that gábdde," Áddjá says.

Vilda's eyebrows shoot up. "But you always say that."

"Because you're always beautiful. But I do think that gábdde really brings out your wings extra clearly."

Vilda giggles, shaking her head a little. She doesn't feel like a butterfly, exactly. More like a caterpillar, if anything. Soft, clumsy, and underdeveloped.

She hears heavy footsteps on the porch before the front door opens again. Irma runs through the hallway, straight into Áddjá's open arms. She barely seems to notice Vilda and the gábdde. Áddjá kisses the top of Irma's head and says, "Hi, sweetheart."

Irma starts babbling about the crazy horse they made her ride at the stable and how it bolted, and she fell off—and about Klara, who filmed the whole thing and posted it as a story in her feed.

Mom smiles at them. "Áddjá will have to hear more about that some other time. We need to get going, girls."

And just like that, the feeling of resistance returns. Vilda takes a step back, retreating farther into the hallway.

"No, we don't," she objects. "There's no rush."

It's as though her whole being is screaming at her: Don't go home. She doesn't even understand why herself; she can just come back tomorrow. But what if she can't? What if something's about to happen? It feels like it is. No, why is she thinking like that, she can't think like that. She needs to get it together now.

Vilda tries to shake off the sense of impending doom, the anxiety. The thoughts popping into her head scare her. They've already agreed she's coming over again tomorrow. She knows that, so what's the problem?

It occurs to her to simply refuse. To sit down on the floor so they have to drag her out.

But Áddjá strokes her arm and says: "Listen to your mother."

So she listens, even though every cell in her body protests.

IRMA'S IN THE front seat before Vilda has even made it to the car. She turns, smiling smugly at Vilda in the backseat.

Vilda rolls her eyes. "What?"

"Just admit it, you wanted to sit up front."

"Why would I even care?"

"Girls," Mom admonishes.

As they exit Áddjá's driveway, Vilda turns around, watching his house through the back window until it's out of sight. She can't explain why her chest feels so heavy. Why she's already missing Áddjá so much it hurts, even though she was just with him. And even though they'll see each other again soon and she'll learn about making antler knife handles and speaking Sámi.

She has to squeeze her eyes shut. Tears are burning behind her eyelids. But she can't cry here, in front of Mom and Irma. They'd probably think something horrible has happened.

BURN. BUOLLET.
Butterfly. Biejvvelådde. Die. Jábmet.
Love. Gieresvuohta.
Even though the words are new in her mouth, they feel like they belong there. She whispers. Doesn't want anyone to overhear.

All evening, she flips through the Lule Sámi dictionary. Looking up words at random and writing them down. The book's cover is slightly worn and there's a loose page inside.

Mom has highlighted certain words. The once neon-pink ink has faded, become watery and pale.

Vilda ponders what to say to Áddjá the next time they see each other. If she's brave enough to say anything at all. No, she has to be brave enough, they've agreed now. But what if Áddjá says things she doesn't know how to respond to, even if she understands? She has to come up with a really good sentence that will make him happy, regardless of how the rest goes.

She works on several ideas in the notes app on her phone. The sentence needs to be big and warm and full of love. And it can't be too simple; she wants Áddjá to be impressed when he hears it.

Her hands are so warm they almost stick to the paper. She flips to the letter H, letting her eyes rove past *headache* and *healer*. Stopping at *heart*. There are two words for heart in Sámi. *Vájmmo* is for when you're talking about feelings and love. A figurative heart, it says. When you mean the bodily organ, it's called *tsåhke*.

Vilda isn't sure which heart she means. What's the difference? All the things she wants to say to Áddjá are both emotional and physical. She can feel them as clearly in her actual heart as in her emotions. Can't she?

It might not matter, because the moment she tries to form a sentence, she realizes the grammar's too difficult. How do you say in my heart, to my heart, my heart? The dictionary doesn't tell her that. Vilda needs Áddjá's help. She can't wait to see him again, can't wait for him to start teaching her. Then she'll finally know what to say. She just has to hold on a little while longer.

She makes a note on her phone: *Tsåhke jali vájmmo.* Heart or heart.

Then she touches the message icon at the bottom of the screen and opens her text conversation with Áddjá. Writes the one Sámi phrase she's absolutely sure about and hits Send.

Mån ähtsáv duv.

He replies in seconds.

Ja mån duv, gieres manna.

She notices that he's made some spelling mistakes, but that's okay. Áddjá doesn't need to be a perfect speller for Vilda to know he loves her, too.

6

THE MOMENT SHE wakes up, she knows she was right: something has happened. She can tell from the silence. No percolator sighing, no plates clattering, no fridge beeping the way it does when Irma inevitably takes too long to decide what to have for breakfast. No TV murmuring, either. Just low, muffled voices. A phone ringing, Mom getting up so quickly her chair scrapes against the floor. Her footsteps and a door closing behind her.

Something has happened, but Vilda's too afraid to try to guess what it might be.

No lights are on outside her room. Not that they need to be. The mornings are bright this time of year, but the sky is overcast and the whole house feels gray. Different. Irma's door is closed; maybe she's still asleep. What time is it anyway?

Dad's sitting at the kitchen table. He drinks from his cup, then winces as he puts it back down. He doesn't seem to notice Vilda at first. She doesn't know if she should make herself some breakfast. The kitchen counter's completely empty. The table, too.

"Hello?" she says.

Dad jumps, as though she's snapped him out of a dream.

"Hi, sweetheart," he says. "A bit early for you to be up, isn't it?"

"What's going on?"

"What?"

"Where's Mom? Why haven't you had breakfast? You haven't even turned on any lights!"

"Sweetheart, sit down, I'll explain."

She sits. Dad seems to be feeling sorry for her; the look in his eyes makes her panic. Why isn't he saying anything? He was supposed to explain. What could be so hard to explain that no words come out?

Vilda wants to scream. Say it! Say it! *Say it!*

"It's Áddjá," Dad finally says.

Hearing those words confirms what Vilda somehow already knew. As though Dad's words give that knowledge permission to burst out, crashing against every nerve and bone, leveling everything in its path.

But only on the inside. On the outside, Vilda's completely calm. "What about Áddjá?"

Suddenly, Mom's in the doorway. Both Vilda and Dad look at her. The only sounds are two bikes zipping past outside the kitchen window and Irma's bed creaking as she gets up. Mom's silence feels unbearable, suffocating. Just looking at her, it's obvious something's terribly wrong. The way she's drooping, the way her free hand is shaking. The other is clutching her phone so hard the screen might crack at any moment.

Mom's voice isn't a voice anymore, more of a noise, but it sounds as though she's whimpering *no. No,* no, no. Vilda has never in her life heard a more horrible sound. It slices clean through her heart.

Then Mom deflates. She crumples onto the floor, as though her skeleton has dissolved. Dad is next to her in an instant, on his knees, taking her hand in his. Vilda just stares, nothing's happening inside her right now. Everything's still. Quiet and still, as though someone had pushed Pause. As though all her feelings, all the new shoots that had just begun to unfurl inside her, are suddenly frozen. Petrified. Dead.

It feels like she should be crying. She wants to cry. Why isn't she crying? What's wrong with her?

What's really going on?

Then Irma's in the doorway. Her hair is bushy and disheveled, like troll hair, and she's still wearing her sleep T-shirt from Dad's work. She rubs her squinting eyes.

"What's going on?"

Dad quickly stands back up, leaving Mom where she is. Irma's eyes are alert now, taking in the family.

"Come here, darling." Dad sits down heavily on a chair and waves Irma over. She takes a seat next to him, pulling her T-shirt over her bare knees.

"It's Áddjá's heart," he continues. "It's been poorly for a while. Early this morning, when he went outside, he . . . His neighbor had to call an ambulance. He's on his way to Sunderbyn now."

Sunderbyn. But that's hours away. They're taking him there? Vilda wants to say so many things, but no words come out. She's mute. She stares at Mom, curled up on the floor, arms shaking. It doesn't even look like Mom. She could just as easily be a stranger, someone none of them knows.

Irma has grabbed hold of Dad's hand. She's squeezing it so hard it looks like it hurts.

In a tiny voice, she asks: "Is he going to die?"

And Dad answers: "It looks that way, sweetie."

7

IT WAS ÁDDJÁ'S heart that killed him. He was in his garden, mowing the lawn, when the pain struck. Abruptly, with no warning at all. He couldn't walk, couldn't stand. His neighbor spotted him through the window and called for help. He had a bad heart, the doctors tell them. Vilda doesn't like it when they say that. There was nothing bad about Áddjá's heart—quite the opposite.

Only now does she understand the difference between tsåhke and vájmmo, between the internal organ and a person's figurative heart. Áddjá's tsåhke was bad. Never ever his vájmmo.

The Lule Sámi dictionary is still sitting on her desk. All the words—Áddjá's words—are preserved, encapsulated, inside its covers. She's afraid to look at them, afraid she'll never use them. Never say them aloud. It's too late now; she has no one to talk to anyway. Mom has always said she doesn't speak Sámi, and Irma doesn't seem to care.

An unexpected certainty, so unthinkable her heart seizes: Vilda's never going to learn her real mother tongue, her family language. Áddjá took it to his grave.

She texts Alma, telling her what happened. Suddenly, it's as though a dam has burst. There's no stopping the words rushing out of her. Not even in her diary has she written as much. She gives Alma a detailed account of everything that's happened—where they were sitting when they received the final phone call, exactly what Dad told them after he hung up, the way Irma's screams made the walls cave in and Vilda's entire body shatter. There isn't room for all the things she wants to write. Grief doesn't fit into a Snapchat message.

Two hours later, Alma replies. By sending a picture, instead of writing in the chat.

She's wearing a straw hat and sunglasses, there's a tall palm tree in the background. Her face is tanned, the corners of her mouth pulled down. Across the photo, she's written: *Oh no, that's terrible!*

Vilda just stares at the picture. How could Alma send something like that, seconds after reading what Vilda wrote? They can usually talk about everything, absolutely everything. But not this, apparently. Did Alma even read her message properly?

Vilda drops her phone, turns over in bed, and buries her face in her pillow. Screaming silently. A warm wetness in her mouth. For the first time since they had the news, she cries, until every muscle in her body aches, until there are no more tears.

Apparently, you can run out of tears. She didn't know that. Eyes *can* run dry. It makes crying hurt even more, like when you keep throwing up even after your stomach's empty. The only thing that comes out are panting gasps.

Later that evening, Dad pops his head into the bathroom when Vilda and Irma brush their teeth. "You're still up?"

"There's no school," Vilda replies. Then she spits out her toothpaste.

Dad nods and pushes past them, taking a seat on the toilet lid, looking heavier than usual. It's as though everyone in the family has grown heavier, somehow. As though it takes effort for them not to crumble.

All day, they've lain in bed or sat on the sofa, crying and hugging. No one has had the energy to pack for their trip to Sundsvall—Dad has already cancelled their train tickets.

It's surreal to think that Áddjá died today. How can they even be brushing their teeth knowing that? Just like before, as though nothing's happened. It's weird how their lives go on after his life has ended.

Vilda rinses off her toothbrush. It's pink with scraggly, worn-out bristles. Irma still has her electric toothbrush with Minions on it, even though she's about to turn eleven. The tiny yellow creatures are hidden behind her fingers when she brushes.

"Can you leave now?" Vilda looks pointedly at the toilet.

Irma spits slowly, if you can even call it spitting—she barely opens her mouth, letting the toothpaste dribble into the washbasin.

Dad has started cutting his toenails with scissors.

"Hello? I need to pee."

She has to push Dad off the toilet. Irma's not as easily overcome; she shoves back with her hip. Just as it's about to come to blows, Dad says: "We should let your sister pee in peace, Irma."

When he shuts the door behind them, Vilda sinks onto the toilet seat. She leans her elbows on her thighs, staring at the wall, thinking about him. Áddjá. Trying to remember all the times he was happy, all the times he laughed. The lilt in his voice when he spoke Sámi. The way he hugged Vilda hard, his hand in her hair.

She tears off a piece of toilet paper and wipes between her legs. Just as she's about to drop the wad of tissue in the toilet, she notices that it's brown. She goes rigid. She peed, nothing else.

Heart racing, she leans forward and looks.

There's a stain in her underpants. Not red, more like a dark brown. For a minute, she just sits there, staring. She's been waiting for that stain, wondering when it would turn up, but now, she suddenly doesn't know what to do. In the end, she pulls off the panties and pushes them deep into the laundry bin, as far down as they'll go. Deep enough to make sure no one will see them.

THE NEXT DAY, Mom knocks on Vilda's door.

"Sweetheart," she says. "Could you come out, I'd like to talk to you." Vilda can tell from her tone what it's about. She tries to keep the corners of her mouth, her whole face, under control, pretending her cheeks are not growing hot. They go to the bathroom. Her underpants are splayed on top of the washing machine, pale blue with a dark stain in the crotch.

"Those are yours, right?"

Vilda mumbles something. Stares at the floor. There are hairs on it, long and tangled. "It's your first time, right? Getting your first period at your age is completely normal. I'm sure some of the other girls in your class have already—"

"Mom, I know!"

"I'm sorry. I'm sure you've learned all about it in school."

"Gee, you think?"

Mom smiles gently, but her eyes look different than before. Two deep pits of grief, even when she's smiling. Vilda's scared to look into them for too long. If she falls in, she might never be able to climb back out.

"Are you in pain?"

"Not really." At least not the kind Mom means.

"Okay, but you tell me if you are. I know from personal experience how rough it can be." Mom points to the cabinet behind her. "I put some pads on the top shelf. Would you like me to show you how to use them?"

Vilda shakes her head, pushing the hairs on the floor around with her big toe. She can't deal with all the questions.

"Can you leave now?"

Mom nods. "But call me if you want me to come back. Okay?"

"Okay."

Before she closes the door behind her, Mom says: "You can choose anything you want for dinner today."

VILDA HAS A shoebox hidden under her bed. Before pulling it out, she closes the door and sits down with her back to it, in case someone tries to walk in without knocking. In the box are a handful of panty liners she received in the post several years ago. A tiny cube of tampons. It's still wrapped in shiny plastic; she's had no reason to open it. There's also a thin, pink pamphlet she was given in school, about love, periods, and sex. Their teacher didn't say anything when she handed them out, just placed one on every girl's desk during a science lesson in sixth grade. Alma already had her period then. The pamphlets quickly disappeared into schoolbags. The boys had wanted to know what they were. Vilda had refused to show them hers.

She folds the pale blue underpants and puts them in the box. They're clean now—the bloodstain's gone. She's not really sure why she's saving them, but it's something she's been planning for years. Now, she can't understand why twelve-year-old Vilda was so eager to get her first period. What did she think was going to happen? For some reason, she had an idea in her head that it would be a grand event. A rite of passage. But that's not how it feels today.

Is she a woman now? She doesn't know, doesn't know anything anymore. As though something's been lost, a piece of reality.

There's no comprehending the fact that Áddjá's dead. There's no comprehending the fact that he will never come back, that he will never teach Vilda Sámi, that she will never have an áddjá to visit after school again. And no Áddjá to try on gábde with, carve knife handles with, or go out to feed the reindeer with. All his warmth and love and care, gone. It's incomprehensible.

She picks up the pink pamphlet. Flips past illustrations of the anatomy of the vagina, hearts, drops of blood, breasts, and flowers. The paper is slick and shiny. On the last few pages, there are questions from teenagers and answers from experts. Someone asks if you can buy a boy flowers to show you love him. Someone else wants to know how to put on a condom. One of the subject lines is printed in big, red letters. It spans the entire width of the page: I'M SO IN LOVE I THINK I'M GOING TO DIE!

Vilda has a hard time imagining what being in love feels like. Especially now. How will she ever feel something good again? When Alma talks about guys, she sounds so excited, as though the mere thought of them makes her giggly. It doesn't feel like Vilda will ever experience that feeling. It feels like she's going to be sad from now on.

She pushes the shoebox back under her bed. Makes sure it's completely out of sight before she leaves her room.

VILDA AND IRMA are sitting in the grass by the lilac bushes. Irma's prodding at Vilda's birthmark—a large, dark brown spot on her arm. Pushing on it as though it were a button. Vilda slaps her hand away, doesn't want her sister's cotton-candy-sticky fingers on her skin.

"Do you have tampons now?" Irma asks. "In one of those pretty boxes?"

"What are you talking about?"

"I thought maybe I could have the box when it's empty? If it's one of those with zebra stripes and flowers?"

"I don't have any tampons."

"I could use it for crafts or something. Or were you going to keep it yourself?"

"I told you, I don't have any tampons. Are you slow or something?"

Irma's eyebrows are fine, faint shadows against her soft skin.

"I heard you and Mom talking about periods in the bathroom. I heard you got yours."

"Seriously, what's wrong with you? Where do you get off eavesdropping on me and Mom?"

"My panties were sticky a few days ago," Irma says. One of the corners of her mouth is twitching. "Mom said it might be discharge. It could mean I'm about to get my period soon, too."

Vilda stands up, brushing the grass off her denim shorts. She can't understand why Irma wants to talk about stuff like this. Especially now, so soon after Áddjá died.

"Like I care."

Irma's eyes narrow. "I'm going to be as big as you soon."

"I'll always be older than you. All our lives, as a matter of fact."

"Only three years older. That's not a lot when you're old, like eighty and eighty-three."

Vilda crosses her arms. She doesn't want to think about being old, being eighty with a failing heart.

"I'm a teenager, you're a child."

"Meh, you're a child, too. You're a child until you're eighteen."

"No, I'm not."

"Besides, thirteen-year-olds are smelly."

"I'm actually about to turn fourteen."

"Then you'll be even smellier."

"Can you stop!"

Irma moves in next to Vilda and sticks her nose into Vilda's armpit. Then she pulls a disgusted face and backs away.

"Ew," she says. "I was right, you reek!"

WHEN A PERSON dies, there are certain things that need to be taken care of in the days that follow. That's what Mom says, as though she's been through the same thing a thousand times before, as though Áddjá was just another person. A dead person's garbage has to be taken out, their fridge has to be cleaned out, their plants watered. Their mail needs to be collected, and leftover medication has to be returned to the pharmacy. Vilda wonders what they do with the medicine. If they give it to someone else or throw it away. She thinks about Áddjá's pill organizer with the little compartments, one for each day of the week. Monday, red. Tuesday, yellow. Wednesday, green. A few pills in each one.

She wonders if he had time to take his Thursday pills before his heart failed.

Dad drives the car to Áddjá's house. Mom keeps her face averted, staring out the window. Irma plays games on her phone; jaunty music can be heard over the sounds of the car. Vilda sits quietly, her hands in fists. She doesn't know what she's going to find when they get there. Never before has she gone into a house that used to feel like home, where no one lives any longer.

When they step into the hallway, the first thing Vilda sees are the shoes. First, a pair of boots, and next to them two navy crocs. She steps out of her own shoes, placing them next to Áddjá's. His are almost twice as big.

Mom and Irma linger in the hallway, sniffling and sobbing with their arms around each other. Vilda pushes past them, doesn't want to get stuck in the darkness.

Walking through Áddjá's rooms, it's easy to imagine that he didn't die, that he has just stepped out for a bit. So many things are sitting out. A newspaper on the kitchen table, the remote in the living room, a cardigan thrown over the back of a chair. Mom starts picking through the left-out things, tidying up, but Vilda doesn't know what to do. Should she help? How? With what?

She and Irma sit at the kitchen table instead and watch Dad potter about. He has started to make blodpalt in Áddjá's pot. Vilda shudders when she sees the black dumplings. They look like smeary rocks. Clumps of period blood.

When the family sits down to eat, Mom strokes Vilda's shoulder and whispers, "A bit of extra iron is good for you right now."

Vilda pulls away from Mom's hand, shaking it off like a dog. Wants to shake off her words, too, but they hang in the air. Irma shoots her a cloying look. Why does everyone have to look at her like that all the time? Why can't they just leave her be?

Dad's eyes turn to Vilda, too.

"You're not eating?" he says. "But you love blodpalt."

"No, I don't."

"You used to, anyway, when you were little."

"So?"

Dad makes no reply. He pours milk into his glass and drinks. No, not his glass, Áddjá's glass. Everything in this house belongs to Áddjá. Áddjá's table, Áddjá's chairs, Áddjá's plates. Vilda hates being here without him, with Mom, Dad, and Irma. It doesn't feel right.

Irma makes little sculptures in the butter with the knife.

"It isn't nice to eat blood," she says. "To the animals."

Dad's glass comes down with a bang. "It's also not nice to not even try the food I made for you."

"Oh, please," Vilda mumbles.

"This is what you've been served. It's this or nothing."

Irma pulls a face. "I don't want to eat this."

"Then you can be hungry."

"Patrik," Mom says. Her hand on his upper arm. "We have to be understanding right now. Especially with Vilda."

Irma frowns. "Why especially with Vilda?"

"This is a tough time for all of us," Mom says. "But puberty and the teenage years are hard under the best of circumstances."

"It wasn't so bad," Dad says. "Except when my moped broke."

Mom sighs, shaking her head weakly. "Sometimes I wish all men could try what it's like to be a woman for a month."

"They wouldn't survive that long." Vilda pokes at her food with her fork. Dad looks skeptical. "Seriously!" She cuts a dumpling in half. "You'd probably call an ambulance if you ever found blood in your underwear."

"You should have been there when I cut my big toe," Dad says. "Don't think I've ever seen as much blood as that time."

Mom dabs her lips with a napkin and clears her throat. "Let's remember that we're eating."

"Yes, too much blood talk." Dad takes a bite of his food. "Let's change the subject."

A sudden stabbing feeling in her stomach. Vilda fixes Dad intently. "I guess it's easy to change the subject when it's not your damn crotch gushing blood."

"*Vilda.*" Mom's voice is hard now.

Vilda's eyes burn. She slaps her cutlery down.

"Are you joking? Okay, so now you suddenly don't want to talk about it, but who brought it up in the first place? You two! Who made you the bosses of what we talk about?"

"It doesn't matter who brought up what," Mom says. "Let's just talk about something else."

"Except apparently, it does matter! You get to talk about how I'm feeling whenever you want without even asking me, but when *I* want to say something on the exact same subject, it's gross. You wanted to talk about my period, so I did!"

"Calm down, sweetheart," Dad says. He keeps scarfing down his food as though nothing's going on. Vilda's so revolted she wants to vomit. Right onto her plate: brown, smeary goop.

"You suck," she says. Her chair scrapes against the floor when she gets up and leaves the table.

Áddjá's bathroom still smells of his aftershave. Vilda locks the door behind her and collapses onto the toilet lid. As she does, the tears come. Her body shakes, shivers; she screams without sound until her jaw aches.

Áddjá's things are still on the shelf above the washbasin. His extra-strength lotion for chapped hands, a bottle of green, mint-flavored mouthwash, a drinking glass with a worn toothbrush in it. She touches the bristles. An overwhelming feeling flares up; it's so big and strong she has to lie down.

She stares at the ceiling, gasping for air. Her tears soak into the bathroom rug, pool in her ears. When she closes her eyes, she can feel someone's hands in her hair. Bony, dry, warm. Áddjá's.

"My darling butterfly," he whispers, so quietly she can barely hear it. His voice makes Vilda shudder.

One of Áddjá's hands moves down to Vilda's face, wiping a tear from her cheek. She smiles. Focuses on the feeling of Áddjá's skin against her own.

A tap on the door makes her eyes pop open.

"Are you in there, sweetheart?" Dad asks from the other side of the door. "I'm not sure why you got so upset, but maybe we can talk about it?"

Vilda ignores him, focusing on slowing her breathing, which is suddenly rapid and shallow. She tries to find her way back to Áddjá, but he's gone.

Dad keeps knocking, a rat-tat-tat against the door, until, in the end, she can't take it anymore. She unlocks it. Avoids Dad's eyes as she slips past him.

10

WHEN THEY'RE DONE eating, they do the washing up in Áddjá's sink. Dad throws out expired crème fraîche from the fridge, pours away a plastic bottle of homemade rhubarb cordial.

"You could have saved that." Mom looks at Dad as though she's disappointed in him. "Why did you pour it out? The girls might have wanted some."

But Dad just shakes his head and keeps clearing out food. Vilda sits at the kitchen table, scrolling on her phone. Irma's upstairs. Her stomping feet can be heard through the ceiling. She sounds surprisingly heavy.

"Vilda," Mom says, turning around. "Do you think you could help me dry?"

Vilda dries the dishes with Áddjá's kitchen towel. Wipes Áddjá's pot and Áddjá's plates, puts everything back into Áddjá's cupboards. She's careful about returning things to their rightful places. Back where they belong, where they've always gone.

Dad is doing the opposite. He's taking all kinds of things out of the cupboards, sorting them, rinsing them, and tossing them. He empties the fridge, the pantry, peeks into the freezer.

Suddenly, Mom drops a plate into the sink so hard the metal clangs. Then she falls to her knees, her hands in the garbage.

"Mom, what are you doing?"

She fishes out a bunch of brown bananas, placing them gently on the floor. Her arms are shaking.

"Katarina." Dad puts a hand on Mom's shoulder. "Maybe you should take a break."

She doesn't listen. Instead, she digs out more things: an old loaf of bread, a bag of oranges with gray eyes. Dad grabs her under the arms and hauls her to her feet.

"Now," he says, more harshly this time. He sounds like he's talking to a dog.

Vilda's still squatting next to the stove, by the cupboard where the pots go. The floor vibrates beneath her feet when Mom strides out of the room. She stomps even louder than Irma.

While Dad cleans out the kitchen and Mom's upstairs with Irma, Vilda goes into the living room. The sunlight's like a yellow filter over the bookshelves. She runs a finger across the spines of the books, stopping at a black one that sticks out a little, as though Áddjá didn't push it back in properly. Three-year diary, it says on the cover. Her heart skips a beat when she opens the book and sees Áddjá's handwriting, preserved in blue ink.

3 degrees Celsius and sunny. Shoveled the roof.

The sofa creaks when Vilda sits. She flips through the book at random, skimming the pages. Áddjá wrote one or a few lines every day for the past few years. It looks more like a logbook than the type of diary Vilda keeps. Short notations, no descriptions.

Girls stopped by. "Trick or treat."

She slams the book shut and hides it under a cushion when Mom appears in the doorway. Her face looks ten years older than it did half an hour ago.

"What are you up to?"

"Nothing, waiting for you."

"We're leaving in a minute—you can wait in the car if you want."

Once Mom's gone, Vilda presses the diary against her stomach, doing her best to cover it with her arm as she hurries outside. She's not really sure why, but it feels like the others would ask her about it if she didn't. And then Irma might want to read it, too, or Mom. Then Vilda wouldn't have it to herself anymore.

For some reason, it feels very important that the diary's just for her.

THAT NIGHT, ALONE in her room, she takes Áddjá's diary out of the desk drawer, where she hid it. She opens it from the back this time, wanting to read his last entry. At first, she's met by blank pages. So many empty, white days that will never be filled. Can she really do this? It almost hurts too much.

The day before his heart attack, Áddjá wrote: *Vilda, my darling child, came by to try on gábde. She looks so much like her áhkko. Must be better about speaking Sámi with her.*

She doesn't realize she's crying until a wet stain engulfs Áddjá's words. She slams the diary shut and wipes her face with her sleeve. The fabric comes away wet and smeared with snot.

How is she supposed to get by without Áddjá? She can't for the life of her understand it.

12

MOM WANTS TO go to Gällivare to buy some new dresses for Monday. When she puts it that way, it makes it sound like Monday's just any old day, or even a fun day. Someone's birthday, maybe. Certainly not the day of a funeral. It might be nice to get away and do something, Mom says. The past few days have been a swirl of grief, tears, and conversations with the undertaker.

Vilda's walking down the stairs when her phone rings. She stops, leaning against the banister. Erica's name lights up the screen.

"Hello?"

"You picked up! I thought you'd died or something. Haven't you seen my snaps?"

Vilda finds herself lost for words. Erica has no idea what's happened—so far, Vilda has told only Alma. Should she tell her now? Explain why she hasn't been responding? But recalling Alma's reaction, it just feels too hard. Erica probably wouldn't understand how awful Vilda's feeling.

It's only when Erica says "Hello?" that Vilda realizes she hasn't responded.

"I've just been busy."

"Okay," Erica sounds vaguely skeptical. "Want to go down to Notudden for a swim in a bit? If we're lucky, Johannes and Lucas might be there, too."

"Johannes and Lucas?"

"You know, from eighth grade. Or well, I guess they'll be in ninth grade after the summer. Whatever, you get who I mean, right?"

Yes, Vilda does get who she means. What she doesn't get is why Erica would be hanging out with them. They're not exactly friends with the guys in the year above.

"I can't," she says. "We're going into Gällivare today."

The relief at having a concrete reason to say no makes her pulse slow ever so slightly.

Because what would she even say if they met up? It doesn't feel like she'd be able to act normally. Especially if they were hanging out with Johannes and Lucas. Why does Erica always insist on inviting people they barely know? Smaller groups are always better.

"All right, maybe I'll ask Siri, then," Erica says. "But let's do something soon, okay? I'm away tomorrow, but can you come over on Monday?"

And just like that, the anxiety rushes back, filling her entire body with aching worry. She pictures Áddjá's dead body, imagines it being lowered into the ground and left there. She tries to keep her voice steady when she replies, "I don't know. Maybe."

"Text me when you know, okay?"

"Mm."

After hanging up, Vilda notices her hand is slick with sweat. She wipes it on her thigh before hurrying out of the house and into the car.

She sits in the backseat next to Irma, staring out the window at the dark landscape. It feels like there's thunder in the air. The anxiety triggered by her conversation with Erica lingers, and Vilda has no idea what to do now. Will she ever be able to hang out with her friends again? She probably doesn't have time to see Erica on Monday anyway, whether she wants to or not. Or does she? Come to think of it, she has no idea what Monday's going to be like. She's been to only one funeral before, but she was little then and can't remember what it was like. What's going to happen?

She googles it and ends up on a website with an FAQ about funerals. Vilda isn't sure what she'd expected, but each question pokes a small hole in her chest. Many of them hadn't even crossed her mind. One reads: *Can the deceased have their own duvet and pillow in the coffin?*

Vilda swipes up the answer with her thumb.

A coffin typically comes with a mattress, a thin duvet, and a pillow, in a range of qualities and styles. The deceased's own duvet and pillow can of course also be placed in the coffin. A burial gown is sometimes included with the purchase of a coffin, but it's also common to use the deceased's own clothing, for example a suit or dress, pajamas, or a nightshirt.

She drops her phone into her lap. Irma glances over at her, but Vilda avoids her eyes, turning away as much as she can, resting her cheek against the seat. Blinking to hold back the tears. Try as she might, the image of Áddjá won't go away. Áddjá on a mattress in his own pajamas, under a thin duvet, trapped in a dark coffin, deep underground. Cold and alone.

When they get to Gällivare, they have Thai food for lunch. Afterward, they stroll through the town center, buying popsicles that melt in the humid heat. As they pass a clothing shop, Irma points to a waistcoat and exclaims, "Áddjá had one almost exactly like that!"

Irma stops to take a closer look, and Mom walks over and puts her arm around her. They say something to each other that Vilda doesn't hear. She doesn't want to stop, doesn't want to look at the waistcoat. What she wants is to keep walking until everything around her is unfamiliar and new, until nothing reminds her of the fact that Áddjá's dead.

Once Irma's done looking, they continue their walk. Suddenly, she blurts out, "I dream about Áddjá almost every night. And in my dreams, we play Ludo like we used to when I was at his house."

Mom pulls Irma close, stroking her hair. She closes her eyes for a moment before answering. "That's lovely." Then she turns to Vilda. "Do you have dreams about Áddjá, too?"

Vilda shakes her head. She feels annoyed but doesn't fully understand why.

Annoyed at Irma for dreaming about Áddjá. About there having been times when Irma was at Áddjá's house without her and they played Ludo together. Just the two of them, without Vilda.

"Why would I?"

Mom gives her a long look but says nothing.

They go into one of the shops. Mom talks about dresses and funeral clothes, but Vilda doesn't listen. Instead, she moves toward a part of the shop she's never gone near before, furtively glancing back at Mom and Irma in the children's section. She reaches out and touches several black lace bras. Pinches the padding. One of the labels says: *Super push-up.* Underneath are matching panties with a very narrow crotch.

She glances back at the children's section one more time before snatching up one of the bras and dashing over to the fitting rooms.

Her own bra is purple and soft with a floral print. She hangs it on a hook and puts on the black one. It's too big. There's a gap between the bra and her breasts. The cups are hard and rigid, not at all as malleable as her usual ones.

What Vilda sees in the mirror is not what she expected. Her body is flat in the wrong places, soft in the wrong places. She looks like a child. Anyone can see she has no business wearing a bra like this. Is she blind or just stupid?

Just as she's about to undo the hooks, she hears Mom's footsteps on the other side of the curtain.

"How are you getting on, sweetheart? Have you found something?"

Vilda drops the bra on the floor. Her hands shake when she picks it back up. "No. Well, maybe."

"Can I have a look?"

Vilda shakes her head before realizing Mom can't see her. "No, it didn't look good on."

She pulls on her floral-print bra and top and manages to wrestle the black bra back onto its hanger. She watches Mom's shoes through the gap under the curtain. They back up a few steps, then she leans against the wall. The rack where you hang up clothes after trying them on is right behind her. Vilda waits. Heart pounding.

When Irma calls for Mom, the shoes disappear from sight. Vilda peeks out. As quickly as humanly possible, she hangs up the bra on the rack next to a black dress, pulls her hair forward over her shoulders and straightens her top.

Mom closes the curtain to Irma's fitting room and studies Vilda. "It didn't fit?"

She shakes her head.

"Want me to get you another size? Or a different model? They have quite a lot of black dresses. One of the other ones might fit better? Did you see the one with the ruffles?"

"Nope."

"Would you like to go have a look?"

Vilda shakes her head again, staring at the floor. There's a grimy piece of a gummy in front of her; she prods it with the toe of her shoe.

"Excuse me?" Mom says. Not as though she didn't hear what Vilda said, more like she's incredulous.

What part of no doesn't she understand? Why would Vilda want a dress with ruffles?

"I just don't want to!"

Mom sighs. "It would be nice if you could find something to wear on Monday, since we've come all the way here."

"I have black clothes at home."

Irma steps out of her fitting room. She's wearing a dark dress from the children's section, with a small gold heart on the chest.

"Does it fit?"

Irma nods and spins around, like she's on a catwalk. Vilda rolls her eyes, grinding the gummy into the floor.

"All right, go get changed and I'll pay for it. Would you like to wait in the car, Vilda?"

She would. Mom gives her the keys and Vilda leaves the shop. The car exhales when she opens the door, and the black seat burns her thighs. She gets into the front, even though she was in the back on the way here. Puts her feet up on the dashboard and pulls out her phone.

Irma throws open the door to the seat behind Vilda, throwing her shopping bag in before climbing in after it.

"Are you even allowed to sit up front?"

"Come off it."

Mom gets into the driver's seat.

"Put your feet down and buckle your seat belt; we're leaving."

Vilda sighs and takes her feet off the dashboard. Mom starts the car and reverses out of the parking lot. It feels like she's looking more at Vilda than the road. Maybe they'll drive into a ditch or crash into a tree and the whole car will explode.

That idea doesn't feel as horrible as it sounds.

13

THEY PLAY ÁDDJÁ'S favorite song at the funeral. It's not a sad song—if anything, it's actually happy and hopeful—but Vilda knows she's never going to be able to listen to it again. From now on, it will ooze jet-black grief. Irma's clinging to Mom's arm. Dad's hands are folded in his lap. No one's hugging Vilda. She's too old to need comforting.

Dad, Vilda, and Irma are the only people dressed in black. Most people, including Mom, are wearing gábde. The many shades of blue light up the church. Vilda considered wearing Áhkko's gábdde, but she was too afraid to ask Mom if it was okay. She would probably have said no anyway. After all, wearing a woman's wedding clothes the day her husband is put into the ground is pretty dark. And not just any woman—Áhkko.

Somehow, it feels even worse now that Vilda's sitting there in her black dress, as though she doesn't belong at her own grandfather's funeral. She stares at the metal buckles on her shoes. Doesn't want anyone to look her in the eye, to notice the truth burning on her face.

The family goes up to place flowers on the coffin. Vilda stays in her seat. If she were to stand, her legs would snap. She's sure of it. She scared to even breathe; a long crack is spreading through her rib cage. If she sits absolutely still, she might survive.

Mom takes her hand and leads her all the way outside. The twilight of the church is replaced by blinding sunlight. It feels reassuring that the sun's still there. Vilda's hugged but doesn't see by whom; her hair is stroked, but not for long enough. Her body grows cold when she's released, despite the summer heat.

They drive over to the cemetery. Dad, Mom's cousins, and a guy Vilda doesn't recognize carry the coffin from the hearse to the grave. Vilda, Irma, and Mom walk behind it. Everyone else follows behind them in a long line. A lot of people knew Áddjá, but no one could ever miss him like Vilda does.

She can't think about Áddjá anymore, but she still does. She can't think about his hands in her hair, how dry they felt against the skin of her forehead. Can't think about Áddjá's laugh. Irma used to blow raspberries against Vilda's stomach, bubbling fart noises that made Áddjá laugh until he cried. He used to have to take off his glasses and wipe his eyes.

She can't think about the fact that Áddjá's never going to laugh again, so she studies the unknown guy instead. He doesn't look like an adult, exactly, not like the other men, but he must be at least a few years older than her. A breeze runs gentle fingers through his hair, making his gábdde flutter.

She can't think about the fact that it's Áddjá lying in the coffin that's about to be lowered into the ground, so she focuses on the unknown guy's hands. His back, his shoulders, his neck. His clenched jaw. His hair that's refusing to settle back down. Her stomach feels strange when she looks at him. As though something's taking root and growing.

They reach the grave. It's marked with a wooden cross; Áddjá doesn't have a headstone yet. Vilda shudders when she sees the deep, rectangular hole in the ground. It's much bigger than she'd pictured. Something inside her is pulling her toward it.

Mom puts her hands on Vilda's shoulders and squeezes.

The coffin is lowered into the grave. Someone gives a speech, or maybe several people do. Vilda doesn't hear. The contours of the world are blurring, blending together like watercolors. The sun's still shining, but it doesn't feel good anymore. How can it still be shining? At a funeral and everything. Doesn't it get that Áddjá's dead?

Áddjá's dead. Dead, dead, dead. How is the sky not getting that?

Someone leads Vilda away from the grave. They all walk away together—she can just about make out other people's backs in front of her. Suddenly, she pulls up short. Mom and Irma take several more steps before they notice.

Mom turns to Vilda. "What's the matter, sweetheart?"

She shakes her head. Shakes and shakes and shakes. Using every last bit of strength she has to keep her feelings inside.

But when Mom puts her arms around her, she can't do it anymore. Every muscle in her body quivers. She sobs, drooling on Mom's shoulder. Clutching the fabric of Mom's gábdde, pressing herself into her.

"My darling, precious angel."

Mom holds her until the worst is over. Eventually, her muscles run out of strength, and her eyes, too. There's nothing left. Vilda wishes Mom would carry her, hug her into her chest, but she doesn't. Instead, she takes Vilda's right hand.

Irma takes Vilda's left, interlacing their fingers.

Her entire body feels empty, weak, and fragile. And yet, she somehow feels a bit better.

"All right, girls," Mom says, seeking eye contact. Vilda can tell she's been crying, too—red, swollen eyelids and a glistening iris underneath. "We're going to head over to the restaurant now, have a nice meal, and then we'll go home. Does that sound okay?"

Vilda doesn't know how anything's ever going to be okay again, but she nods. Mom hugs them both so tightly Vilda's nose presses against Irma's. Their breaths mingle. Become one. Vilda tries to smile, but Irma doesn't.

The moment they step into the restaurant, the sun calls it quits. The sky has run out of strength, too. It rumbles, cracks, and opens.

14

HE'S SITTING AT the next table. Sipping coffee instead of a fizzy drink, tapping away at his phone with quick thumbs. If he were to look up at any point, their eyes would meet. He hasn't so far, but she's hoping, wishing. Waiting. Even though she has wanted to hide ever since they got to the church, she wants him to see her now. Only him.

The priest is seated at the same table as Vilda's immediate family. He asks her about school, seemingly forgetting that it's summer. He's heard that Vilda's good at drawing; his eldest is as well. Dad answers for her. Nodding politely in the right places. Mom downs cup after cup of black coffee.

The guy smiles at something on his phone. The sight makes the corners of Vilda's mouth twitch, too, for the first time in many days. When she takes a closer look at his gábdde, she realizes it looks a lot like Áddjá's. Almost exactly the same, in fact—dark midnight-blue with a paler sliehppá. There are squares of red, yellow, green, and blue around the collar, between edges of white reindeer skin.

His gábdde makes Vilda think about Áhkko and Áddjá's wedding photo. They were so young back then. Suddenly, she catches herself picturing the guy at the next table marrying her, what their wedding photo would look like. The thought makes her face burn, forcing her to look down, away. How can she think about love when she's supposed to be grieving?

Irma pokes Vilda. Whispers: "Who's that?"

She jumps. "Who?"

"That guy," Irma says. "The one you're staring at."

"How should I know?"

Vilda notices Dad putting a hand on Mom's shoulder and giving it a light squeeze.

Then he turns to them. "Ready to go?"

Before they can reply, Mom has picked up her handbag. They stand up and thank the priest. Vilda runs both hands through her hair, smoothing it down. She runs a fingernail over her eyebrows and glances back at the other table.

The chair he was sitting in is empty.

She looks around, but there's no sign of him. The room's packed. A muffled din fills it. Mom, Dad, and Irma disappear through the door, but Vilda doesn't move. She picks up her glass bottle, drinking the last of her fizzy drink. Sticky raspberry coats her lips. She scans the room, needing to see him one last time.

Just as she's about to give up, she spots him. He's standing with his back to her, talking to someone, but she can tell from the posture and hair that it's him. Two tassels dangle from the belt around his waist. She has a sudden urge to touch them, to run her fingers through the strands.

An older lady bumps into Vilda, knocking the bottle out of her hands. It shatters against the floor, sending glass flying in every direction. The guy turns around, his eyes sweeping across the floor and up toward Vilda. For the first time, their eyes meet.

She'd pictured the moment differently. Now, she's standing there with burning cheeks and a broken bottle on the floor in front of her, laid bare to his gaze. The mortification of being caught is almost too profound to handle.

She dashes toward the exit, leaving the broken bottle. Pushes the door open and bursts outside. A rich smell of warm rain. The air too thick to breathe. She can still feel the guy's eyes on her skin, and she has goose bumps under her dress.

Just then, she spots a butterfly fluttering right in front of her. It's completely, completely white. For a second, she stops and looks at it, overcome with a sudden serenity. All the way from the restaurant to the car, the butterfly remains by her side.

Irma gives her sister a searching look as Vilda climbs in and buckles her seat belt. "Ready?" Dad asks, looking at them through the rearview mirror.

"Mm."

"Then let's go."

They sit in silence until Mom reaches back and strokes Vilda's knee. "I'm so proud of the two of you."

"Why?" Irma asks.

"You did so well today. My beautiful, strong girls."

Vilda doesn't have it in her to respond. She rests her cheek against the seat and stares out the window.

"Who was the guy who carried the coffin?" Irma asks.

Dad signals a right turn. "Which one?"

"The one who wasn't an old man, obviously."

Vilda looks at Dad. He's focused on the road.

"You mean Samuel?" he asks.

Irma leans forward between the seats. "How am I supposed to know?"

"Oh, you recognize Samuel, don't you?" Mom says. "His dad, Nils-Johan, and Áddjá were close. They worked together with the reindeer. You used to play with Samuel up in the mountains."

"Whatever, he wasn't big then. He looks like an adult now, almost."

"I suppose he is. Seventeen, I think. Or is he about to turn eighteen?"

"Why did he get to carry the coffin instead of us?"

"I don't know, honey." The familiar sound of crunching gravel as they turn into the driveway. "He stepped up."

It's even warmer outside the car than inside it. When Vilda gets up to her room, she takes off all her clothes—dress, tights, and shoes. Leaves them in a pile on the floor. Wearing nothing but panties, she throws herself on her bed. The bedspread is cool against her sweaty skin.

What is she supposed to do now? What is she supposed to do now that the funeral is over and Áddjá has been put in the ground and everyone is done hugging? Now that the priest has said his piece, and everyone has cried and offered their condolences. Now that the tears have stopped. Is it done now? Is it over?

It doesn't feel like it's over to Vilda. It feels like this is when it all begins.

15

A FEW DAYS later, she runs into Samuel again. Vilda, Irma, and Dad are together at the shops when it happens. They're buying ice cream, fruit, and cheese doodles for their Friday movie night. While the others choose what to have for dinner, Vilda gets to do the pick and mix, and that's where she spots him. He has a phone wedged between his shoulder and his ear, twisting his arm into strange angles to reach. Almost everything he picks out is black. Licorice fish, salty skulls, chalk bites, and cats.

Vilda doesn't like licorice, but she goes for the same ones anyway.

Samuel looks different than last time—instead of the brightly colored gábdde, he's wearing worn jeans and a brown leather jacket. It looks warm. Vilda notices now that he has a birthmark above his eyebrow, the same color as his jacket and hair. It makes her think of chocolate.

Their hands collide over one of the bins. An electric shock runs through her, crackling in her stomach. Samuel spares her a quick glance, an apologetic smile.

He looked at her. He smiled. What if he recognized her?

He moves over to the other end of the wall of sweets. She can't make out what he's talking about on the phone, but he's definitely speaking Sámi. The prosody opens up something inside her, a longing that seizes her and refuses to let go. What if it's not too late? What if she could speak Sámi with Samuel? He sounds a lot like Áddjá, only younger.

Something about the hoarseness of his voice makes her feel safe.

She wonders who he's talking to. Does he have a girlfriend? Vilda pictures herself as his girlfriend. Imagines being the one he's buying all those sweets for, because tonight they're going to his house to make out on the sofa. She can imagine his tongue in her mouth. The taste of licorice. His warm hand on the back of her neck.

When they're back in the car, she pulls out her phone and opens her mom's Facebook profile. Clicks on her list of friends and searches "Nils-Johan." One match. She opens his profile and searches "Samuel." There are three of them, but she instantly knows which one's the right one. The hair, the eyes, the chiseled jawline.

His surname's the key she needs.

When she opens Instagram, a selfie of Erica pops up in her feed. The realization makes her stomach knot. She'd promised to call Monday, but there was no room for thoughts of Erica then. Should she write something now? Explain that she was at a funeral? She starts typing out a message, but in the end, she deletes it. She has neither the energy nor the words. Plus, if she does contact her, Erica's probably going to want to nail down another day to meet up, and Vilda doesn't want to. She can't bring herself to pretend like everything's normal, not yet. If she just leaves it, Erica might forget they ever talked about meeting up. She has so many other friends to hang out with anyway—she should barely notice Vilda ghosting her.

Vilda clicks the search bar, types in Samuel's full name, and finds a private account. She can't see anything beyond the small, round profile picture. She stares at that for a long time, ignoring thoughts of Erica's pool pictures on Snapchat.

All the way home, she thinks about Samuel's smile, his dark eyes. Rests in that warm feeling. She's not even mad at Irma for taking the front seat.

VILDA USES THE softest, darkest pencil for Samuel's eyes. Shades them with her fingertip, which comes away sooty and black. Dabs with her putty rubber to add a glint to his irises.

She spends hours on the portrait. And yet, something's not quite right; she just can't figure out what it is. Did his nose come out too long? Or are his eyes too close together? It doesn't really look like him, no matter what she does. Maybe there are too many things she doesn't know about Samuel. The pencils clatter when she drops them back into their case.

She flips through her sketch pad. Mom has asked her to do a portrait of Áddjá. To hang up in the living room, so they can always see him. A nice, happy picture. *Because you're so good at drawing.* But Vilda can't, she just can't, even when she tries. Every time, it ends with her covering the entire page with black. Grief has no other shades.

But Samuel. There's a light shining inside him. Her fingers itch when she thinks about him—she has to draw him, record his likeness. Study him. Drawing a person is a little like being close to them. And what Vilda wants most of all right now is to be close to Samuel.

How does the sunlight make his hair gleam?

How many birthmarks does he have on his face, his neck, his hands? How does the skin around his eyes change when he smiles?

She needs to know.

16

"**ISN'T THIS A** book for grown-ups?" Irma asks, flipping through the pages. She's sitting on Vilda's bed with a bag of library books in front of her.

Vilda doesn't answer. She goes to the mirror and dabs lip gloss on her lips. She has almost every flavor lip gloss—her favorites are Coca-Cola, Strawberry Kisses, and Tropical Coconut. Irma's always telling her they're not flavors, *Because you don't eat lip gloss, do you?* But they are. You don't have to swallow to taste them.

She wonders what it would taste like if Samuel kissed her now.

"Seriously," her little sister exclaims from the bed. "This is like what Mom reads."

"Yeah, and?" Vilda puckers her lips at her reflection. "I guess Mom and I have the same taste in books, then."

"How would that work? You're a child."

Vilda rounds on Irma. "Do you have to be in here?"

"Do you have to be so mean?"

"Get out."

Irma falls back into the pillows, settling in with her arms behind her head. "No," she says. "This is my house, too."

"You have your own room."

"It's not as cozy. Can we swap?"

Vilda drops the lip gloss back into her makeup bag. "Never going to happen."

"You're always so grumpy," Irma complains. Her upper body's dangling off the bed now, dangerously close to Vilda's hidden cardboard box. Irma pulls out the bottom drawer of her nightstand. "Is this your diary?"

"What do you think you're doing?"

Vilda leaps across the room, grabbing Irma's arm and pulling her up off the bed.

"Ow!"

"Get out, now!" Vilda insists.

Irma snorts derisively, suddenly completely unperturbed by Vilda's hand around her arm. "You sound like a toddler."

"How do I sound like a toddler? I said three completely normal words."

Irma twists her mouth into a sad clown face, mimicking her. "*Get out, now!*"

Vilda grabs both her upper arms and starts shoving her toward the door. Irma's socks reluctantly slide across the floor.

"We have our own rooms for a reason. I can't deal with you being in here all the time, you stupid muppet."

"*Mom!*" Irma shouts. Using all her weight to stay put. "Vilda's calling me a stupid muppet!"

"Now who's the toddler?"

In the end, Irma gives in to Vilda's shoving and staggers the last few steps out of the room. Vilda slams the door shut behind her, wishing she had a key to lock it, too. No, not just a key, something more definitive than that. She wants walls and concrete. A stone wall no one in the whole world can break through.

EVERY NIGHT, IN bed, Vilda reads a few entries in Áddjá's diary. It makes her feel close to him. Almost as if they're talking, or as if he's telling her about his life.

The winter before last, he wrote: *Laid tracks to the new pasture. The girls helped.*

Vilda remembers when she and Irma used to sled behind Áddjá's snowmobile. They'd lie on their stomachs on reindeer skins, close together in their snowsuits, banging their chins whenever the sled went over bumps and rocks. Irma would laugh straight into Vilda's ear, so loudly it hurt. Áddjá would drive even faster than Mom—they got their cheeks scratched if they didn't look out for tree branches. And when they'd leave the forest behind and head out onto the lake, he'd speed up even more. Sometimes they had to stop to pick up Irma's and Vilda's hats when they flew off. Powdery and white with snow.

Sometimes, Vilda likes to fantasize about the day she'll ride snowmobiles with her boyfriend. They could each have one and race across the lake. Or share the same one, her arms around his waist, just like when she rides behind Mom. Except with him, it'll feel completely different. She'll rest her cheek against his back, gazing out at the mountains and forest. Thinking that there can be no greater happiness.

She takes out her phone and searches for Samuel's name on Instagram. In his profile picture, still the only one Vilda can see, Samuel sits on the ground, marking a reindeer calf's ear. He's wearing a gray jacket and a black baseball cap. His bio's two words long: *Állosujtár Jåhkåmåhkes*. It's a thrill to realize she understands what it means without having to look up the words: *Reindeer herder from Jokkmokk*.

He has seventy-three posts. She can't see any of them, but that's what it says. Seventy-three pictures: that's an awful lot compared with how few she's seen.

She hesitates, her thumb hovering above the blue Follow button. Then she touches it, and the button changes color from blue to white. Requested. A surge rushes through her body, so sudden and overwhelming that she has to turn over in bed, push her face into her pillow, and kick her legs around a little. The feeling crackles all the way out to her toes.

Her blind is down, but a ray of midnight sun has managed to find its way into her room. Vilda pushes herself up into sitting position, crawls to the window, and snaps the blind open. The light comes flooding in so suddenly and harshly she has to close her eyes against the shock of it. Then she slowly opens them again, letting the sunlight trickle in slowly. It fills every part of her body until there's no room left for darkness.

18

JUST AS THE doors to the supermarket slide open in front of Vilda, she hears someone calling her name.

"Vilda! There you are!"

She looks around, confused at first. Then she spots Erica, waving from the parking lot. She's sitting on the hood of a maroon A-Traktor, surrounded by several girls from their class as well as Johannes and Lucas, the about-to-be ninth graders. Now, she regrets not writing to Erica—coming up with an excuse feels a lot more difficult in real life than on Snapchat.

It occurs to her that she hasn't talked to a single person from school since Áddjá died. And that even though she's used to seeing them every day, it feels weird now. As though she doesn't quite recognize them. Or is she the one who has changed?

"Seriously, where have you been?"

She considers making a run for it. Ignoring them, ducking into the supermarket, pretending not to have heard. But she's already looked over—it's too late to run. She takes a few steps toward the group, trying to smile, except she can't seem to keep the corners of her mouth up. They're so much heavier than usual.

"Hi," she says. Then, instantly regrets it—what kind of reply is that? But Erica doesn't seem to care.

"What are you up to?" she asks. Smacking sounds come from her mouth, where a white piece of gum rolls around. "Getting groceries, or what?"

Vilda nods. "You?"

"We were going to take the A-Traktor out for a spin. Johannes turned fifteen a few weeks ago and got his license."

"Cool, sounds fun."

Vilda glances over at Johannes and Lucas, once again failing to understand why Erica is suddenly hanging out with them. Not that she should be surprised. If anyone was going to make new friends over the summer, it would be Erica.

Johannes waves his junior driver's license around, grinning broadly. "Hop in if you want to come with."

"Is there really room for everyone?"

"Yes!" Erica shouts. "We want to hang out with you!"

Vilda frantically casts about for an excuse, but before she can come up with one, Erica has pulled her into the car.

Johannes drives through the roundabouts on the main street, turning around in the last one to let the cars lined up behind him pass. While he drives, he cracks bad jokes that make Erica laugh out loud. They go up and down the street several times. Vilda is closest to the door in the backseat, wedged in next to Siri from her class. Siri's long hair falls across Vilda's shoulder.

There are far too many of them in the A-Traktor. Vilda can't understand why they always want one more person to join, why Erica always wants as many friends around her as possible. And she doesn't know how to act around these people. Siri joined

Vilda's class in seventh grade, and so far, she has spent most of her time with the other people who attended the Sámi school. Not with Vilda, Alma, Erica, or any of the other girls. She's not sure they've ever actually talked to each other outside of group assignments at school. Now, Erica keeps showing Siri things on her phone. They giggle so hard they're snorting.

"Have you seen this one?"

Erica holds up her phone to show a meme. It's a picture of a person driving a snowmobile with two guys on a snow racer sled behind it, captioned: *Reindeer herding with today's fuel prices.*

"Is that true?"

"Kind of." Siri chuckles.

Erica's gaze turns from Siri to Vilda. It takes her a few seconds to realize Erica's waiting for her to answer.

"I mean, I don't have any reindeer," she says.

"But your family does, right? I've heard you and Irma talk about it. You know, reindeer markings, or whatever it's called."

"Sure."

"Your grandpa works with stuff like that, doesn't he?"

Something about the way Erica talks about Áddjá in the present tense makes Vilda's anxiety flare back up again. She tries to beat back her thoughts. She can't let grief swallow her now—not here, not with everyone looking. They'd never understand.

"Wait a minute," Siri suddenly exclaims. "Ábmut's your granddad?"

Vilda only has time to nod before Johannes locks eyes with her in the rearview mirror.

"Hold on, what?" he says. "*You're* Sámi?"

"Mm," she replies. Hesitates. "Why do you sound so surprised?"

He shrugs, shooting her an uninterested smile. "You just don't look it."

Lucas, who's in the passenger seat next to Johannes, laughs. And then everyone else does, too. How can Erica laugh at that? Didn't she think it was mean? She seems to find everything Johannes says hilarious now. What's with her? She wasn't like this around him before the summer break.

Siri seems to be the only one who doesn't think Johannes's comment was hysterical. Vilda glances over at her, and for a split second, their eyes meet. Siri's mouth is slightly open, as though she's about to say something, but she doesn't.

Vilda has never given any real thought to what a Sámi person looks like. She doesn't have a gábdde, doesn't speak the language, but the way she looks? She pictures Samuel's face. Does he look more Sámi than her? Did Áddjá? She doesn't know.

She wants to ask Johannes what he means, but she doesn't. She can tell from the guys' hissing laughter that they'd probably keep mocking her if given the chance. She wishes someone would tell them off, defend her. But there's no one like that here.

Something vibrates against Vilda's arm. Siri pulls her phone out of her jacket pocket.

"Hi," she says. Then she's quiet for a while. "Iv mån diede. Gánnu ávtsen."

Siri's speaking softly, but Vilda's sitting too close not to hear. She stares out the window, focusing on the houses and buildings.

Siri continues to answer in Sámi. She sounds slightly annoyed. Vilda takes out her phone, holding it close to her chest so no one can see the screen. In her notes app, she writes down the words she catches from Siri's conversation. Not because she wants to know what Siri's saying, but because she wants to learn the words. She's thrilled when she manages to catch entire sentences, because they have word order, sentence structure, grammar. Not from a book, but from a real conversation. She wants to remember what a girl her age sounds like.

After hanging up, Siri looks over at Vilda, who almost drops her phone on the floor. She quickly locks the screen, smooths out her face, and does her best to look casual. But Siri doesn't look suspicious—in fact, she's smiling. Then she leans forward between the seats and says: "Turn it up!"

Johannes turns the music up so high it feels like they're sitting inside a loudspeaker. Vilda's whole body tenses up. She has to keep telling herself to relax. Unclench her jaw. She unlocks her phone again, using it to escape.

That's when she notices: Samuel has approved her request to follow him.

"Hey, what are you smiling about?"

She shakes her head at Erica's question. Has to yell to make herself heard. "Nothing."

Vilda turns as far toward the door as she's able. Her heart's pounding and thumping; she's filled with an urge to run and jump. The feeling's fizzing inside her, like carbonation in her bloodstream.

When she clicks Samuel's name, she notices that her thumb is trembling. Not just her thumb, actually, her entire hand. It's ridiculous, really. What's happening to her? This feeling in her body is so new. She can't remember ever being this happy.

She eagerly scrolls through his feed. She can see everything now: all his posts, all his photos. Samuel on a snowmobile at Easter, the frozen lake behind him glittering in the sunlight. An Arctic char in the snow next to a tin of snus. More fish from various seasons; a herd of reindeer being released back into the mountains after an earmarking night. It looks beautiful. And Samuel is so, so beautiful, too.

She scrolls back up, realizing as she does that one of his most recent posts is an autumn picture. Does he post that rarely? She clicks the photo to have a closer look. It was posted two weeks ago, not last autumn.

In the picture, Samuel and some other people are sitting around a fire in a reddish brown landscape. An ATV parked next to them. A dog, a handful of lassos, and a cooler scattered in the underbrush around them.

And there, at the edge of the photo, is Áddjá, holding a gukse.

Rest in peace, Ábmut, one of the most knowledgeable reindeer keepers I've ever met.

We'll miss you in the mountains.

She can't push down her feelings anymore, or her thoughts; try as she might, she can't run. It doesn't matter that Vilda was happy a second ago, because Áddjá's dead and never coming back. The pain will always, always find her again, wherever she hides—when she least expects it.

She had no idea Samuel and Áddjá were close enough to make Samuel miss him.

Samuel barely existed before the funeral, at least not in Vilda's world.

She struggles to regain control, wants to seem normal in front of her friends, but it's already too late. Grief is in charge now. Nausea pushes up through her throat—she feels cold and sweaty at the same time. There's no air in the A-Traktor. She has to get out. Now, now, now.

"Stop."

No one hears her; the music and the guys' laughter drown every other sound. "You have to stop! Pull over!"

She pushes open the car door and staggers out onto the pavement. Doesn't care that people are calling after her. There's a pain in her chest. What if it's her heart? It feels like it's her heart.

Just then, her phone dings in her hand. Samuel is following her back.

ERICA'S NAME APPEARS on her screen. She writes: *Seriously, what happened? Are you okay?*

Vilda spins around in her desk chair, hesitating for a moment before replying. For a split second, she considers telling Erica how she's feeling, instead of pretending everything's fine. It would feel good to confide in someone about her grief and about Áddjá. But if even Alma can't understand what it's like for Vilda, why would Erica? The two of them have never been as close as Vilda and Alma, even though they've been in the same class at school for years.

Just period cramps.

Erica's reply is virtually instantaneous: *Aw, poor you! Wanna hang? I can come over in like fifteen minutes.*

Vilda's briefly terrified that Erica might drag the whole gang over to her house, but she shakes off that thought. She did write "I." And something about her message makes Vilda wish things were like before again. That they were still in seventh grade and hung out sometimes after school. It wasn't usually just the two of them, but it did happen. They'd make smoothies at Erica's house and watch scary TV shows, the kind Vilda's parents won't let her watch. Erica's parents were away on work trips a lot, sometimes for days on end, and because Erica's an only child there was no one to stop them or tell them no. Vilda used to be jealous of Erica being left home alone so often. It seemed pretty great to be left to your own devices, with no family to bother you.

In an attempt to hold on to the feeling that everything's normal, Vilda replies: *Okay, fun!*

Mom and Dad seem over-the-top happy that Vilda's having someone over. They greet Erica as though they haven't seen her in ages, even though it really hasn't been very long.

Erica doesn't look annoyed by their curiosity, though; she happily answers their many, many questions. She even gives Vilda's mom a hug. Then Vilda drags her away, and they shut themselves in her room.

At first, they can't think of anything to do. Erica tells her everything that's happened since school ended, but mostly she talks about Johannes. How cool he is to let everyone ride in his new A-Traktor, and how fit he's become. Vilda can't understand how she can like someone so obnoxious, but she keeps that to herself. She doesn't have much to contribute to the conversation. Besides, it's hard to act like you're having period cramps when you barely know what that feels like. From time to time, she puts a hand on her stomach and winces, hoping it comes off as believable.

"We could put on makeup?" Erica suggests at length.

"Except I have, like, no makeup," Vilda replies. "Just lip gloss and stuff like that."

Erica pulls a small, black makeup bag from the tote she threw on Vilda's bed. "Always prepared," she says. "I don't think I've ever seen you with makeup on, have I? I bet you'll look amazing."

It's immediately obvious that Vilda's not used to having makeup put on. Her eyelids twitch when Erica applies the eye shadow; she blinks several times when the mascara brush approaches her lashes. It's as though her face doesn't want anything to do with any of it. Erica changes the song on Spotify so often it makes Vilda's body itch with restlessness.

Vilda studies her face in the mirror. Watches Erica's makeup brush sweep across her cheeks, turning them faintly pink. She wonders what Johannes meant by his comment. *You just don't look like one.* What if he's right? After all, very few people at school realize that Vilda's Sámi. What if that's not just because of the language and the gábdde, but because of the way she looks, too?

"Do you think I look Sámi?"

Vilda's surprised to realize she's asked the question aloud. Erica briefly lowers the brush, studying her face in the mirror.

"Hm, I don't know," she says. "You and Siri don't exactly look alike." A tiny crack in her heart.

"But I don't really know what a Sámi person's *supposed* to look like. Neither one of you look like that singer guy, Jon Henrik."

"Jon Henrik's adopted from South America."

"Aha." Erica puts the brush down, studying her creation. Dabs some highlighter on the tip of Vilda's nose. "But seriously, here's what I don't get. Why didn't you go to Sámi school, if you're Sámi? Like Siri and the others."

Vilda tries to ignore the feeling ripping and burning inside her. It feels like she's about to burst into tears again, but she refuses to give in. Not with Erica looking. She's already acted weird enough for one day.

"I honestly don't know. My parents picked my school, not me."

....

"Mm. Just seems kind of weird. But hey, don't you have one of those gábde, then? Siri wore hers to the last day of school ceremony, it was dead gorgeous!"

"I do," Vilda mumbles. Swallowing and swallowing and swallowing.

"Really? Can you put it on, so I can see?"

For the first time since Áddjá died, Vilda pulls on Áhkko's wedding gábdde. She can't reach back far enough to tie the sliehppá on properly, and she has a hard time pulling the gábdde over her head, too. Everything gets tangled; she has to ask Erica for help.

"Damn, girl!" Erica exclaims after Vilda smooths down her hair and buckles the belt around her waist. "You look incredible!"

Vilda has to smile. Erica's eyes linger on her lips; she looks thoughtful. Then she pulls a small bottle out of her toiletry kit.

"This lip gloss is almost exactly the same color as the red on your gábdde," she says. "Let's try it on."

Vilda puckers her lips so Erica can paint them. Some ends up outside her lip line, so she wipes it off hard with toilet paper.

When Vilda sees her reflection, she actually does look better than she'd thought she would. The red on her lips is bold and bright. Her eyelashes look almost twice as long; they stick together a little when she blinks. Somehow, her eyes seem to have grown bigger.

She wonders what Samuel would think if he saw her now, wearing her gábdde.

They put makeup on Erica, too, but since Vilda's fairly clueless, Erica has to do most of it herself. They take a couple of selfies together, but Vilda waits until after Erica leaves to try to take properly nice pictures. For some reason, she looks different on camera than she does in the mirror. Not as good-looking. If she turns to face the window, her eyes look brighter, but the background comes out uneven—you can see her desk chair, the pile of clothes thrown over the back of it, the porcelain cat next to her lava lamp. She tries leaning against her wardrobe door, taking her film poster down so the background's all white. Gray shadows slither across her face.

Nothing works. After taking hundreds of photos from every conceivable angle and in every conceivable light, she ends up choosing one of the first ones. She ups the contrast but blurs the background. Dials up the colors until the gábdde looks as blazingly blue as it does in real life. Her lips and eyelids glow.

When she posts the picture to her Instagram, she guesses she actually does look a bit older than usual. You might think Vilda's a girl who has kissed several guys, who has a boyfriend, even. A girl who has spoken Sámi all her life, takes it for granted.

Surely no one can tell her she doesn't look Sámi now?

She adds some hashtags in Swedish, Sámi, and English. Wants as many people as possible to see her now. The moment the picture is posted, she lies down on her bed and drops the phone next to her. Afraid to check if she's getting any likes. Or comments. My god, what if someone comments? Normally, it's mostly Alma writing stuff. Or her grandpa on Dad's side, a few days after the fact.

What if someone comments. What if Samuel comments.

In the end, she can't stop herself. She unlocks the phone, scrolling through her notifications. She actually has had a few comments. She's thrilled, until she notices the most recent one, from Johannes, the soon-to-be ninth grader.

Now you look Sámi :)

Vilda barely has time to react before she sees the next comment. An American man who didn't follow her before has left a comment: *Beautiful!*

Before she's done reading that one word, another comment appears. Another stranger, who writes, *Sámi girls are hot. Snap?*

She turns over on her bed and stares at the wall. Touches the end of a sleeve, trying to unravel the feelings that have become tangled up inside her gábdde. To think that a piece of clothing and some makeup can make that kind of difference. That it can make guys see her. Is that what it takes to look Sámi, like Johannes said?

Eventually, there's a comment from Alma. She writes: *Insanely GORGEOUS!*

Followed by several lines of hearts and emojis.

Vilda realizes she's smiling. She feels a bit bad now about not having liked any of Alma's recent pictures. The truth is she's been unsure if they're still as close as before. That's why she's just kept scrolling when Alma's pictures have appeared in her feed, trying to shake off that bitter feeling. Alma barely seemed to care when Vilda told her how awful she felt after Áddjá died. Can you really be best friends after that?

She's not used to doubting their friendship. They've always been close—closer than close. Twins, soul mates, all of that and more. Like sisters, Alma likes to say, but that's just because she doesn't have a sister. Only brothers. If she'd had a sister, she would have known they're a pain, more often than not. But Alma's not a pain, she never has been. The only real fight they've ever had was in nursery school, over an apple or a shovel or a rock they'd found in the woods. Neither one of them can actually remember what it was about—that's how unimportant it was.

Now, it feels like a lifetime since Vilda last saw Alma. As though they were completely different people then. And in a way, it was a lifetime ago—Áddjá's life, and part of Vilda died with him. Nothing's ever going to be the same again.

She double-checks to see if Samuel has liked the picture, but he hasn't. Of course he hasn't. What had she expected? That Samuel would notice her just because she's wearing a gábdde? That's normal in his world.

She can't even be bothered to yell at her sister when Irma comes barging into her room, landing on the desk chair. It creaks slightly as she scoots across the floor.

"Why are you wearing a gábdde?"

"Why not?"

Irma shrugs. "If you could choose, would you rather be a boy or a girl?"

Vilda sighs into her pillow. "Boy."

"What, why?"

"Isn't it completely obvious? Everything about being a girl sucks."

"Give me one example."

Vilda glares at Irma. She sounds like she's fifty or something.

"Periods, that's one. Or giving birth. Do you realize that guys, like, don't ever experience that kind of pain?"

Irma has reached the dresser now. She picks up the porcelain cat, pressing its pink nose against her own. "I bet they do when they die."

"Probably not even then."

Vilda peeks at her phone. Seven more likes.

"When you get older, you're going to get how awful bleeding from between your legs is."

The porcelain cat ends up in the wrong place when Irma puts it back down. Then she starts fiddling with some white rocks Vilda brought back from the mountains.

"Okay, but imagine how gross it would be to have a penis," Irma says. "Even if it doesn't bleed."

Vilda snorts. "True. That's actually grosser."

She glances down at her phone again. The reactions on Instagram keep coming. She opens the picture, looking at it for the hundredth time. The gábdde and her red lips. She almost doesn't recognize herself, but at the same time it feels like her true self. The person she wants to be.

"Did you feel weird about us not wearing gábde to the funeral?"

Irma holds up two of the stones to her face, like eyes. "Weird how?"

Vilda shrugs even though she's lying down. Puts a hand under her pillow. "Don't know. Maybe because it looked like we're not Sámi when, like, everyone else was wearing gábde."

Irma frowns. Starts scooting back toward the desk. "I guess, but . . . It's not your clothes that make you Sámi, right? You're the same person inside, no matter what you wear."

"I just felt like we didn't fit in."

"I think Áddjá would be sad if he heard you."

The shame comes suddenly, without knocking, ripping the door off its hinges and barging in. Vilda has never thought about it that way. Would Áddjá be upset with her? Once the thought's in her head, she can't erase it.

She hates that Irma said that. And she hates it even more that Irma's probably right. At the same time, her words are soothing. If Áddjá would have been sad, that means Vilda's wrong. And if she's wrong, that means she *did* belong at the funeral, as much as anyone else. That she's enough.

A green, fuzzy frog hits Vilda in the head. "Hello?" says Irma, who's thrown it at her. "You never asked me what I would choose!"

Vilda pulls the frog close, hugs it to her chest. Its eyes stick out like balls. She should really have got rid of it a long time ago, but it's too cute to throw out.

"What?"

"Boy or girl."

"Fine, so which would you choose?"

"Girl," Irma says. "I feel a bit sorry for all the boys who have to be boys. It must be such a pointless existence."

Fifty-year-old Irma is back. Vilda has to smile, and when she does, something suddenly glitters inside her, a giggle that won't be held back. Irma doesn't hesitate for a second before she attacks. She lunges at Vilda, tickling her neck, her armpits, her stomach folds. The buckles on Vilda's gábdde jingle. Irma's a ruthless tickler, downright brutal.

Then the mood fades, and Irma curls up next to Vilda. Like the porcelain cat, only soft and warm. They lie there in silence for a while. Vilda feels Irma's breathing in her own body.

"I hope I die before you," Irma says.

Vilda flinches. "Why would you say that?"

"So I never have to live without you."

Irma's neck is warm against Vilda's nose. She snuggles in closer. When Irma wears a tank top, you can tell that her tan starts right below the shoulder and goes all the way out to her fingertips.

"Well, I'm a lot older than you," Vilda says. "So I'll probably die first."

"When you're old and sick, three years is, like, nothing."

"But why would you be sicker than me?"

Irma pulls out of Vilda's arms, stands up. She shakes herself like a dog.

"A person's heart can break at any time," she says.

26

AS VILDA TRIES to sneak past the living room to get to the bathroom, she's spotted by Mom.

"Wow!" she exclaims from the sofa and stops typing on the computer on her lap. "Are you going to a wedding?"

Vilda sighs. "No, I just wanted to take a picture."

"A picture? What for?"

"Just a picture, okay!"

Mom waves Vilda over, and she reluctantly approaches the sofa. "Are you wearing makeup?"

"Yes."

"You don't usually wear makeup, do you?"

Vilda perches on the armrest. "Erica wanted us to put on makeup, so we did."

"I see," Mom says, closing the laptop. "You do know you don't have to put on makeup just because she wants you to, though, right?"

What's with the third degree? Vilda doesn't understand why Mom even cares. "Well, maybe I wanted to as well. Have you ever considered that?"

Mom shakes her head a little. "Well, you look lovely. The gábdde suits you."

"Okay, thanks."

Vilda gets up but pauses in the doorway. She turns to Mom, who has opened her laptop again.

"Why didn't I go to the Sámi school?"

Mom looks up. "Huh?"

"Well, I'm Sámi, so why didn't I go to the Sámi school?"

Mom shrugs vaguely. "I guess it started with your preschool. The Sámi preschool is pretty far from here, so we opted for one that was closer, so we could walk. And then I suppose we just figured you'd be happier going to the same school as your friends from preschool."

It irks Vilda that Mom's so blasé all of a sudden. That she keeps tapping away on her computer as though this were no big deal.

"So you didn't think it was relevant that we're Sámi? That *you're* Sámi?"

Mom frowns. "I'm not sure I understand what you're getting at. It's not as if it's the school you go to that determines how Sámi you are."

"Not everyone would agree with that, you know!"

She storms out, back into her bedroom. Falls onto her bed with her face in her pillow.

After a while, she hears Mom entering and sitting down on the edge of the bed.

"Vilda," Mom says in her gentlest voice. "Who's been telling you you're not Sámi because you didn't go to the Sámi school?"

"Like, everyone," she mutters.

"Oh, sweetheart." Mom strokes her hair, pushing a wayward strand back behind Vilda's ear. "You know that's not true. Are the people who are saying this to you Sámi themselves?"

"No."

"No, exactly. So they don't know what they're talking about. Why would you let them define how Sámi you are?"

Vilda hasn't thought about it that way. But on the other hand, it's not as simple as Mom is making it sound. Can Vilda really be Sámi if other people don't understand or believe that she is?

"My little bunny," Mom says, getting up from the bed. "Don't forget to wash the makeup off later."

And just like that, she goes from wise to annoying. "I won't."

"Good."

Mom leaves Vilda deep in thought. She should really talk this through with someone who's Sámi themselves and knows what the deal is. She knows one person who'd be perfect. A person she'd love to get to know better and who has everything Vilda lacks— the language, the reindeer, his own gábdde. Besides, they have quite a few things in common.

A dizzying thought: imagine all the things Samuel could teach her if they got together. They could speak Sámi with each other, like she and Áddjá were supposed to do, and she could get involved with the reindeer in earnest. Participate in the earmarking and the herd splitting like she used to with Áddjá sometimes. With her and Samuel following each other on Instagram, she's already one step closer.

A bright, bright feeling of hope.

21

SHE HAS READ Johannes's comment so many times she knows it by heart. His friend Lucas has liked it, but other than that, it's drawn no reaction.

She clicks Reply. Is she really going to respond? Yes. She is. She does it quickly, before she can talk herself out of it.

It's not my clothes that make me Sámi. Or the way I look.

She doesn't know what she'd expected—applause, tons of likes, or a hostile comeback—but nothing happens. Several minutes go by. Then several hours. But she actually feels okay about it. In fact, she feels pretty good. For once, she believes in herself.

Late that night, she has a notification about someone liking her comment. But it's not Johannes, or someone from her class.

It's Samuel.

22

VILDA AND IRMA spread their towels out on the grass next to the public pool. Dad takes a seat in a plastic chair. His face is sunburned—when he pushes his sunglasses into his hair, you can see the much paler skin around his eyes. Dad doesn't really tan—he turns bright red. His nose has taken the brunt of it this time. Vilda's own nose hurts just looking at him.

They already have their bathing suits on under their dresses. Irma pulls her dress off, throws it at Dad, and races barefoot toward the pool.

"Careful!" he calls out. "It's slippery!"

She does a cannonball. The children closest to the pool get splashed.

Vilda takes her time, kicking off her crocs; the grass is prickly under her feet. Sharp.

She fiddles with her dress, pushing the fabric in under her fingernails.

Dad looks at her from his chair. "You're not getting in?"

She meets his eyes. "No, I am."

He pulls a black paperback out of his bag, a crime novel. The author's name takes up half the front cover. His thumbs press against the pages when he opens it. Once he starts to read, Vilda takes off her dress. Looking around both before and after.

"Be careful, sweetie. It's slippery."

As though she didn't hear him the first time. She steps out onto the wet pavers lining the pool. Then, just as she's about to dive in, her foot slips off the edge and she falls. It's a painful belly flop. The pool swallows her whole, the world around her goes quiet. Her hair swirls around her head; it's all she can see. She hears Irma's voice from somewhere far, far away.

Vilda breaks the surface with a snort. Swallows air. Coughs and spits. Irma comes gliding toward her on a giant inflatable crocodile. She's lying on her stomach, paddling with her arms in the water.

"Have you seen who's here?"

Irma's hair slithers like snakes across her shoulders. A string of snot has wrapped itself across her nose. Vilda can't be bothered to tell her. Instead, she pushes her own hair behind her ears and wipes the water out of her eyes. It stings.

Irma mimes something, but Vilda doesn't understand.

Behind her, she hears the splash of two people jumping into the pool. She turns around and more water sprays into her eyes. There's hooting and laughing when the first of the two comes back up. A broad, tanned back and dark brown hair. It almost looks black when it's wet.

Seeing Samuel makes her jittery. There are so many things she wants to say to him, and this is her chance. She just has to take it.

A second guy resurfaces, snorting and laughing, too. His hair's lighter than Samuel's, but his back looks the same. His shoulders. His body.

Vilda is suddenly uncomfortably aware of her bikini, the pink one with the strawberries. And of Irma, paddling about on her crocodile just a few feet away. She sinks as deep into the water as she can, her chin level with the surface. Doesn't want them to see her, to notice her body.

At the same time, that's exactly what she wants.

Samuel and the other guy start sparring with long foam noodles. The friend takes a blow to the head and sinks into the water, dead, while Samuel laughs and coughs by turn.

Vilda doesn't look away when he turns toward her. He looks straight into her eyes, and she thinks this is it, this is the moment she finds the courage to say something to him. Something in Sámi.

But there's no time, because the formerly dead friend launches out of the water, hurling himself at Samuel with a roar. They splash about wildly.

Even though Vilda's mouth is above water, she can't breathe. The snout of Irma's crocodile bumps the back of her head.

"Play with me. I'm bored."

Vilda considers shoving Irma off to the other end of the pool. Why does her sister have to be here, ruining everything?

"Play with your crocodile."

"Hi," Irma suddenly exclaims loudly. Vilda goes rigid, has to fight an urge to sink to the bottom of the pool and never come back up. Samuel and his friend look around, their eyes on Irma and Vilda for just a handful of seconds before they resume their wrestling. Luckily, they don't seem to have realized Irma was talking to them.

"Boo," Irma says. "No one wants to play with me."

Vilda swims over to the other end of the pool as quickly as she can. Her arms burn, and the water feels heavier than usual. The crocodile follows hard on her heels.

"Do you have to be like that where they can hear you?" Vilda asks.

"Like what?"

"You know what I mean!"

Vilda heaves herself onto the ladder, taking more care walking across the pavers this time. Irma climbs out after her.

"Hey," Samuel's voice says behind them. A voice that makes her stomach flip. "I think you dropped these."

Samuel grabs the ladder and holds up a pair of pink goggles. Irma touches her forehead. Bends down and takes the goggles from him.

"Thanks, that's so nice of you!"

But Samuel isn't looking at Irma when she's talking to him. He's looking at Vilda with eyes that make her heart flutter. His eyes slowly slide down from her chin. Her skeleton turns to putty. She's suddenly weak in the knees. Forgets all the words she's been wanting to say to him, in every language.

The water glitters when he swims away.

"That was so nice of him," Irma says as they set off toward their towels.

Vilda makes no reply. She can't think anymore. Her brain has stopped working.

The lawn is full of people now; it's so crowded they have to stop to let a gaggle of children by. They almost stumble into a little girl wrapped in a yellow dressing gown. She's sucking on an orange slice, waving up at Irma and Vilda. Irma waves back.

"Why do you have hair under your arms?"

"Huh?" Irma looks confused until the girl points at Vilda. Her finger glistening with orange juice.

"And on your legs. Like my dad!"

It feels like all eyes turn to Vilda, and there's nowhere for her to hide. Her bikini suddenly feels tiny and see-through. What was she thinking, going out in public dressed like this?

She ignores the girl and tries to keep walking like a normal person, even though her heart is screaming at her to run. She bumps into a few wet shoulders and elbows as she pushes past. Irma follows in silence.

Dad looks up, resting his book in his lap. "Done already?"

Vilda nods, drying herself with her towel. Her feet are covered in grass. She pulls on her dress even though her bikini's still wet underneath. The fabric turns dark, the outline of her bikini soaking through it.

When Dad asks if they want soft-serve, only Irma answers.

23

SHE OPENS THE window, breathing in the smell of grass being cut. An assurance that it's still summer, that there's still grass that needs mowing. That's still growing. Like her. Growing so fast it needs to be stopped, can't let it get too long; it grows like the hair under her arms. On her legs. Between her legs. She doesn't tell Mom she wants to shave. Mom would probably tell her there's no need, that Vilda's too young. But thirteen, almost fourteen, is not as young as Mom seems to think.

Her birthday's in two days. It feels strange to think about, as though time has been passing her by. Normally, she likes to plan for it, enjoying the anticipation, but nothing's normal anymore. This year, she's not looking forward to her birthday, she's scared of it. What will it feel like without Áddjá there? Is everyone going to be sad? It feels like it can't, mustn't, shouldn't be like that.

She locks herself in the bathroom. Takes off her T-shirt, grabs the scissors, and looks at herself in the mirror with her arm folded back. The girl at the pool was right: she really does look like a dad with that dark stuff in her armpits.

Why would Samuel want to be with someone who looks like a dad? What if that's why he looked at her like he did? Because she's an ugly freak. And she didn't say a word, even though she'd been waiting to talk to him. Why didn't she? She might never get a better chance.

Using the scissors in the mirror turns out to be difficult; they keep moving in the wrong direction. And it's even harder when she has to use her left hand. It's impossible. A few severed hairs sprinkle her bare skin.

She sits down on the toilet lid, cold from perspiration. She tries to wipe off the loose hairs with toilet paper. It gets everywhere, even though there's so little of it. Some of the hairs cling to her shorts, others don't want to leave her warm armpit. Some wander down along the side of her stomach.

Why can't they just get off her? Why can't they just leave her alone?

24

SHE SEARCHES FOR Samuel's full name on Spotify. An account appears with the same profile picture as his Instagram. He has twenty-four playlists. Vilda reads some of the names: *Deep Rap, On the Pull, Sámi Pop.* The most recently added list, created just a few days ago, is called *Jshfkgjk*.

It's exactly one song long.

Even though Vilda has decided never to listen to it again, she plays it now. The notes are heavy like grenades; they make something she wants nothing to do with unfold inside her. A map of grief, a reminder of everything that hurts.

It's Áddjá's favorite song. Áddjá's funeral song, in Samuel's most recent Spotify playlist.

Vilda doesn't understand. Does Samuel listen to this song? Does he think about Vilda's áddjá when he does?

It feels like her heart's going to hammer its way out of her chest. It beats and beats and beats, so fast it feels like it might explode and die. No, not die, she doesn't want to think that, but once the thought is there, it won't go away. And no matter what thoughts Vilda may have, Addjá's dead, and nothing can change that. If she were to dig six feet down into the black earth, open the coffin lid, and place a hand on Áddjá's chest, it would be still and cold. If he even has a chest; Vilda has no idea how long it takes for a body to decompose. She squeezes her eyes shut, trying to fend off that image.

It's like pushing a beach ball underwater.

Thoughts crash over her mercilessly. And feelings: fear, grief, shame. She regrets every last horrible image she creates, but she can't stop. The room shakes, the floor, the walls, her bed. The ceiling's going to cave in, she's sure of it, the whole house is going to collapse, and none of them will make it out.

She rips off her headphones and throws the window open, sucking in air. Only now does she hear the rain, pounding against the ground. It sounds like the asphalt might crack.

But the birds are still singing in the trees, as brightly as ever.

She carefully opens her bedroom door. Creeps past Mom and Dad on the sofa in front of the TV, down the creaky stairs. She steps into her crocs, doesn't bother with her raincoat. Slips out through the front door and steps into the downpour.

The sky hurls water at her, or maybe it's tears—that's how it feels when they hit her skin. There's a rumbling above her. Peals and claps of thunder, and suddenly, some of the pressure inside Vilda dissipates. As though her feelings have moved out of her and up into the sky.

Vilda closes her eyes. Samuel's right there behind her eyelids, waiting for her. She really can't understand why he's posting pictures of Áddjá and saving his funeral song on Spotify. Still, she feels closer to him now. As though they share something.

She thinks about Samuel so intensely the pain subsides and her muscles relax. His gábdde, his hair in the wind, his bare back in the pool. The hoarseness in his voice when he speaks Sámi. Her shoulders come down, her fists unfurl. When she opens her eyes again, the rain has stopped. Just like that, as though it never happened. The birds have gone quiet in astonishment.

Thinking about Samuel has made every last raindrop retreat back up into the clouds.

25

SHE TURNS FOURTEEN. Is woken up by Irma crawling into bed with her, pushing her freezing feet in under the duvet. Vilda grunts and pulls herself into a seated position, slumping against the wall. Mom and Dad sing. It's silly that they still sing for her—she's not a child anymore. They put her presents down on the bed. One ends up on Vilda's knee, another on Irma's shoulder.

Irma holds up a slim parcel. "Please, please, please, open this one first." The wrapping paper is a shimmering shade of pink.

Vilma's eyelids are still droopy with sleep, heavy and soft. She rips off the paper, revealing the cover of a sketch pad inside. She smiles with sleepy lips, yawns, says thank you.

"Can you draw me tonight?" Irma asks.

"Nope."

"Come on, I gave you the sketch pad!"

"So, how does it feel to be fourteen?" Dad asks.

Vilda shrugs. Yawns again, covering her mouth with her hand.

"Technically, she's not fourteen yet," Mom says. "Ask her again at 2:42 P.M."

After they leave, Vilda picks up her phone. She's received several birthday messages. Alma has sent a snap of some kind of exotic bird and Erica is wondering when they're going to celebrate. She replies that she's planning to throw a party after the summer—since so many people are away. Deep down inside, she's pretty happy about that, but she's not about to admit it to Erica.

Irma has baked cupcakes. She's made animal faces in the frosting—frogs, cats, and tigers. Vilda eats two for breakfast, and the sugar buzzes inside her.

Mom puts out chips, sweets, and cheese doodles, even though it's not even noon yet.

Dad and Irma sit on the sofa with a big bowl in front of them. Their fingertips are bright orange.

People come, people go. Mostly relatives and some of Dad's friends. They sing and drink coffee and hug, Vilda smiles and thanks them for her presents. When all the guests have left, Irma suddenly asks: "When's Áddjá coming?"

They stare at her. Several seconds go by before something shifts in her eyes. Then, just as suddenly, she bursts into tears. Dad pulls her into his arms, comforting her, stroking her hair. Vilda's heart is racing, but she holds it together. This is her birthday. She's not going to be sad today.

It's like trying to shut an ocean up in a water bottle.

Just before dinner, the doorbell rings again. It's Fanny, Vilda's godmother, and she has brought her new boyfriend. They hand Vilda a black envelope, which she opens with her index finger. A gift card for Kicks in Gällivare. Now she can finally buy some makeup.

The boyfriend's name is Tom, and he gives Vilda a hug even though they've never met before. His arms are strong and soft at the same time, and he holds the hug longer than strangers usually do. She can feel the warmth of his body through his shirt. Smell his cologne. Vilda hides her face against him for a long moment.

Fanny helps Mom cook. Tom's there, too, putting a hand on Fanny's lower back when she's cutting cucumber and tomatoes. He kisses her neck, making her giggle. Vilda can't take her eyes off them.

She offers to cut the pepper. Slowly slices it down the middle, flicking away the seeds one by one. Forcing down her aching grief by imagining Samuel's hand on her waist. His lips behind her ear, tickling her.

"What are you giggling about?" Mom asks. She turns the steaks over, making the pan sizzle.

"Nothing."

"How's that pepper coming along?"

"Good." Vilda tucks one of the seeds under her thumbnail.

"Dinner's almost ready. You're going to have to speed up a bit."

Samuel puts his hand on Vilda's. Interlaces his fingers with hers. He kisses her earlobe, continues down her neck. The hairs on her arms stand up.

"Vilda, I'm getting stressed." Mom takes a tower of plates out of the cupboard. They clatter so harshly Vilda's ears hurt. "Finish cutting that pepper now so we can get the salad on the table."

The racket makes Samuel vanish. Vilda is snapped out of her reverie, yanked back to the crushing pain.

"Cut it yourself, then," she says, dropping the knife on the cutting board. "If you're in such a damn hurry."

Mom heaves a sigh. It's the most annoying sound in the entire world. "I don't understand why you're upset."

"Because you're always on my case!"

"In what way?"

"Like right now! Can't you leave me alone for once?"

"I can't do anything right." Mom puts each plate down on the table with a bang. "Everything I do is wrong."

"I can finish cutting that, Vilda," Tom offers.

Vilda looks down at the cutting board, blinking, blinking. Swallowing her tears, shaking her head.

He gently pushes her aside. "You go do something else for a bit."

So Vilda leaves. She holds it all inside, goes to her room, and shuts the door. Then she takes out Áddjá's three-year diary and flips through the months. Stops when she finds July.

Exactly two years ago, he wrote: *Vilda 12 years old. Birthday party with my darlings.*

Seeing that, Vilda falls apart—grief is a tidal wave that makes her body crack from the inside out. She curls up on her bed, gasping for breath. She cries because she has a mother who doesn't understand anything, because it'll be a hundred years before she's as old as Tom. She cries because Samuel isn't there and maybe never will be. But most of all she cries because of Áddjá. Because he's not there to celebrate her fourteenth birthday. Because he's not comforting her, hugging her, holding her. Because he never will again. Never, ever again.

She picks the book up again, holding it with trembling hands. Tries to remember her twelfth birthday. That was when Áddjá gave her the gukse he'd carved, with Vilda's name and a tiny heart on the handle. Irma got a gift, too, a key ring with a heart-shaped wooden charm. But she was still jealous of Vilda's present. No one in the entire world has a prettier gukse than Vilda.

The memory is a warm light inside that makes her muscles relax.

Outside her door, she hears Mom calling: "Time to eat, Vilda."

She slips into the bathroom first. Splashes freezing water on her face, rubs her eyelids. They're swollen; the redness refuses to go away. Her breathing feels heavy in her chest.

When she gets downstairs, she walks straight into Mom's arms. Mom holds her tight, rocking her gently, kissing Vilda's temple.

"Nothing's quite as it should be, is it?"

Vilda shakes her head and presses herself closer to Mom. Mom heaves a heavy sigh, pushing a few hairs back behind Vilda's ear.

"My darling little birthday girl."

"I'm not little," Vilda mumbles into Mom's shirt.

"Yes, you are," Mom says, stroking her hair. "You're always going to be my little girl, no matter how big you grow."

26

SHE'S SITTING IN the garden with her diary, its cover cold against her bare thighs. Her hair keeps getting in the way, brushing across the pages as the wind plays with the loose strands, making the skirt of her dress flutter.

It's hard to describe Samuel. When she thinks about him, she feels something she's never felt before. She wants to be close to him, really, really close. Wants to feel the warmth of his skin. The feeling is like an ache in her, like something's missing. She doesn't understand why that would be—she's never actually been near him.

She turns the words this way and that, but they come out sounding washed out, as though they've already been used too many times. Everything she writes sounds trite, generic. It could be about anyone she likes. But Samuel isn't just anyone.

"It's nice to see you smiling," Mom says, sitting down in the sun lounger next to Vilda's.

Vilda slams her diary shut. Picks her phone up from the grass and opens a snap from Alma. "What do you mean?"

Alma's eyes are sparkling and much larger than usual. Her lips are pink beneath the filter. In the background, Vilda can see a beach and the turquoise ocean. Apparently, the weather's always good in Cyprus.

"It's just nice that you're happy," Mom says. "Are you texting with someone?"

"Mm, Alma."

"Is she having a good time on Cyprus? She's so lucky to be able to be away for so long."

"Yeah."

Vilda's actually not sure about whether Alma's having a good time, but judging from the pictures, she is. They've barely talked since Áddjá died. Before Alma left, they had almost three hundred straight days on Snapchat. They were trying to get to a full year, but now their streak's ruined. Since they haven't been in touch every day, the counter has started over. Alma still hasn't said anything about Vilda's loss, hasn't even asked how she's doing. Is she simply not going to, ever? Then what will it be like when Alma comes back, especially if Vilda's still sad? She doesn't know if she'll be able to pretend everything's fine.

A notification pops up on her screen—Samuel has posted on Instagram.

"You're smiling again."

"She just wrote something funny."

Mom leans closer so Vilda has to angle her screen away. Mom smells like sunscreen and warm skin. Her insinuating smile bothers Vilda.

"So, how does it feel to be fourteen?"

"Don't know."

"It's big! I remember when I was a teenager."

Vilda turns away from Mom. Holds her phone up close to her face. She clicks her way to Samuel's Instagram account, checking out the picture. It's him and the guy from the pool, leaning against the hood of a blue car, wearing backward baseball caps.

"My *god*, I was so in love with Mikael in the year above me! I wrote pages and pages about him in my diary even though he barely said one word to me. Looking back, I must have been a bit nuts, actually. And then there was Conny, but that was later."

"Hmm."

"When I met your dad, I was nineteen. I've told you about that, haven't I?"

"More than once."

"You don't want to rush things," Mom says. "Love comes when it comes."

Vilda shakes her head without taking her eyes off the screen. She zooms in on Samuel's face. Then she hears the garage door close behind her, Dad's footsteps in the gravel.

"Did I hear you say Conny?"

"Shh!" Mom tries to wave him away. "Girl talk!"

"Jesus," Dad says. "Are you talking about the Conny I work with?"

"You didn't even live here back then."

Vilda gets out of her sun lounger, grabbing her phone, diary, and pen. "Nooo!"

Mom reaches out after her. "Don't leave!"

"I didn't mean to break things up," Dad says.

But Vilda leaves anyway. She hears Mom berating Dad until the door slams shut behind her.

27

DAD'S PLAYING MUSIC on YouTube. The kind of old-timey rock Vilda and Irma call Dad music. It's an apt name, because only dads would ever listen to that kind of music. They don't like Dad music, but right now, they're dancing anyway. Dad's whistling along to the rock ballad's intro, Irma's playing air guitar, and Vilda's on vocals. Dad pulls up his sleeve to show them he has goose bumps.

Mom smiles as she walks by.

The music they're listening to is stuff he liked back when he and Mom met. They were eighteen and nineteen then; she was a year older than him. He was at his first proper music festival, and there, in the audience, he saw her. For Dad, it was love at first sight. But not for Mom. She was cool back then and thought Dad was a bit of a dork.

The hairs on Dad's arms are standing straight up. He points, saying, "Listen, listen to this."

Vilda and Irma listen, but they don't really care about the song. Or at least Vilda doesn't.

Irma grabs her arm, leans in close, and whispers, "Do you think you have to be in love? Isn't it enough if you love your sister?"

"It's not the same," Vilda sneers. "Really not the same."

Irma backs up a little, meeting her eyes. "How would you know? You've never been in love."

Vilda shakes off her little sister's hand. "You seriously think I would tell you if I were?"

When she shuts the door to her bedroom behind her, she can still feel Irma's eyes burning on her back.

28

SHE CAREFULLY OPENS the dictionary, greeting the Sámi words. They're still there, on the pages, just like before Áddjá died.

Seep. Vuohtjot. Shame. Skábmo. Shine. Tjuovggat.

Suddenly, she hears Áddjá's voice. The way he would pronounce the words on the page, exactly the way they would sound coming out of his mouth. They sound nothing like it coming out of hers, but she tries. Testing them out, again and again. It's hard, as though her brain and her tongue aren't connected properly, but she refuses to give up. She keeps repeating the words until her tongue softens. Eventually, they start to sound better, more like they should.

Maybe it's actually possible, this—maybe if she practices every day, she'll be able to speak Sámi like Áddjá. But not with him. Never with him.

She opens Samuel's Instagram account. Clicks one of his selfies and gazes deep into his eyes. Whispers words in Sámi with her eyes locked on his. Her heart flips. Imagine if he could hear her, if he knew. It's what she wants more than anything. Why didn't she say something to him at the pool? That was her chance, especially when he handed her and Irma the goggles.

Maybe she should text him? But it has to be in Sámi, no matter how intimidating that feels. It would likely radically increase the chances of him being interested.

She opens her notes app to jot down some potential texts. Flinches when she reads *tsåhke jali vájmmo*. She deletes the sentence immediately, as though she were swatting at a mosquito. Pushes down the thoughts of never saying anything in Sámi to Áddjá ever again. She's going to say something to Samuel instead.

She opens a new document and stares at the blank white screen. The problem's still the same: she feels unsure of how to put together a sentence. Googling, she finds a Lule Sámi dictionary app, a handful of children's songs, and a PDF with Sámi phrases. Maybe there's something she can use there? She scrolls through the pages, past numbers, colors, months, and greetings. Eventually, she comes across something that might be interesting. *Ij ávvá tjáppemus guovsoj le nåv tjábbe gå dån.* Not even the most beautiful daybreak is as beautiful as you. She has to giggle. Imagine if she sent him that.

She copies down a few phrases:
Mejt dagá? What are you doing?
Mån lav 14 jage vuoras. I'm 14 years old. *Mån åhtsålav duv.* I miss you.

29

A SMALL GREEN dot in the corner of Samuel's profile picture. Vilda stares at it. Her heart beats faster and faster as she opens the chat. Just seeing the message field makes her feel lightheaded. What are they even going to talk about? Music, maybe— she knows what he listens to now. But she didn't actually recognize any of the artists, so no, it'll have to be something else.

The only thing she can think of, that she's sure they have in common, is Áddjá. But what is there to say about him? *Hi Samuel, it's Vilda, I saw you at my grandfather's funeral and noticed you've saved his funeral song on Spotify.* He'd think she was weird. And besides, she's determined to write in Sámi.

She puts her phone down and stares at the ceiling, sighing. Maybe she's overthinking it. Maybe she should just write *hi* and see what happens? Samuel should know who she is. He follows her and even liked one of her comments. That should be enough, shouldn't it?

She wishes she could ask Alma for advice. The thought is completely out of the blue.

Alma doesn't know about Samuel, doesn't really have any idea of what's going on back home, with Vilda. But before, she used to know everything—they both knew everything about each other. Will it ever be like that again?

In the end, she just does it. She writes *hi*, adding a pink flower emoji. Hesitates, changes it to *buoris,* and hits Send before she can change her mind again. She exits the chat as quickly as possible, doesn't want to know if he's reading it, if he's replying. Closes the app. She's mortified and excited, all at once.

The floor creaks behind her when someone enters without knocking. She can tell from the footsteps that it's Dad. Something frigidly cold touches her bare shoulder.

"*Ow,* seriously!"

Dad holds out a popsicle that's still in its wrapper. "Have a Twister."

"Can't you see I'm busy?" She uses her phone to push his arm away.

"It's a *beautiful* day," he says. "You're not going to spend it inside, are you, hunched over your phone?"

"Why don't you go outside and enjoy the beautiful day so I can write to my friends in peace?"

"Finish up and come outside," he says before leaving the room and disappearing downstairs.

Vilda leans her head back against her desk chair, spinning around a few times. Then she unlocks her phone, unable to stop herself. Samuel hasn't replied. But what if he will, soon? Or no, what if he *doesn't* reply? Then what is she going to do? Write again? It's been four minutes now. Only four, but it feels like at least forty. How long should she wait?

She gets up from the chair and walks over to the window. The whole family's out there: Irma's skipping rope on the pavement, Mom's sunbathing, Dad's washing the car. Vilda watches them for a while, making a mental sketch of the scene. She fills the sky with blue, the exact color of Irma's T-shirt. The jump rope is a blurred, vibrating oval around her.

Vilda doesn't understand where Irma finds the energy to skip in this heat. Irma's hair is fluttering, even though there's no wind. She has never been affected by the world around her the way other people are. She's never low because of an overcast day, and she never stays inside just because it's raining. It's as though things like that don't touch her. Irma has her very own weather.

30

MOM'S FINGER TICKLES the sole of her foot.

"You're overheating," she says. "Have a drink."

Vilda pushes herself upright in the sun lounger, only now realizing that her head is throbbing. Mom hands her a plastic cup with a straw. The squash is lukewarm.

"You put on sunscreen, right? On your eyelids, too?"

"Mm."

Vilda closes her eyes again. Farther away, she can hear Irma's jump rope beating against the asphalt.

"It feels like we're abroad," she says. It smells like it, somehow. Not the usual at-home smell of grass and dirt and pine trees, but something new. She doesn't know if the sun has a smell, but if it did, this would be it.

"Yes, isn't it wonderful?"

Vilda's phone dings from under her sun lounger. Sunscreeny fingers smear the screen. Even though the brightness is turned all the way up, she can barely see anything. A few letters. A word. A name that makes her dash barefoot across the gravel driveway, up onto the porch and into the hallway.

Inside, the air is cooler. The rooms look blue before her eyes adjust. Her pulse is pounding as she unlocks the phone again. She reads Samuel's message: *Who?* In Swedish.

A thousand thoughts rush through her mind. He doesn't know who she is? Then why did he follow her back? At least he replied, that's the most important thing. But what should she write? Who is she? What does he want to know?

Vilda sinks down onto the bottom step of the stairs, staring at the message. Can't think of anything clever to say, so in the end, she just writes: *Vilda, haha.* Adding an emoji sticking out its tongue.

This time, the reply is instantaneous.

Vilda?

His questions are making her nervous. How many people named Vilda does he know?

If she just explains, he has to understand, right?

We sort of met at the funeral. And at the pool when you found Irma's goggles.

She sends. Realizes he might not know Irma's called Irma, so she quickly types out another message.

My little sister, Irma, I mean, the one riding the big crocodile.

The moment she hits the Send button, she realizes he really should know that, since they used to play together when they were little. Granted, Vilda and Irma barely remembered that until Mom reminded them, but Samuel probably does. After all, he's older. Now, it almost sounds like she thinks he's stupid. She writes again.

But I guess you know that already since we used to play together in the mountains when we were little.

That sounds so strange, that they used to play together. She heaves a sigh, running her hands over her face. Why does it have to be so hard? The whole thing is almost starting to feel silly.

And yet. She's texting with Samuel, for real, imagine that. She's never been this close.

Three dots next to his picture. Time stands still until his message comes through.

Ok?

This is her chance. Is she going to do it? Yes, she is, she has to do it now. She opens her notes app, checking the phrases she copied down earlier. Something ignites in her stomach, a sparkler set alight.

She writes slowly, one letter at a time.

Mejt dagá?

She hesitates. Double-checks the spelling several times. Isn't this just insane? She's never written to anyone other than Áddjá in Sámi before, and barely to him, either. No one else knows she's trying to learn.

She counts down.

Three.

Two.

One.

It feels like the Send button catches fire when she hits it.

Sunlight floods into the hallway as Irma throws open the front door. She kicks off her sneakers before noticing Vilda.

"What are you doing?"

Vilda locks her phone and puts it down next to her. It feels like it's vibrating against the palm of her hand, but that's just in her mind.

"Nothing."

"Right."

Irma stops in front of the full-length mirror in the hallway. Her T-shirt is riding up slightly, revealing a sliver of belly. She pulls it down.

"You never answer questions anymore."

Vilda frowns. "What's that supposed to mean?"

"I, like, don't know anything about you. Whenever I ask you anything, you snap at me."

"Maybe you should stop asking so many questions, then."

Irma turns to Vilda with an exasperated sigh, meeting her gaze with dark eyes. "I'm not allowed to talk to you, or be with you, or even look at you!"

Vilda gets up, sneaking a peek at her phone to see if Samuel has replied, but he hasn't.

Her phone slides into the pocket of her sweat shorts. "Do whatever you want."

"Like you're the boss of me!"

Vilda can feel Irma's eyes burning on her back as she begins to climb the stairs. After a moment, she hears Irma following.

"If the whole house was on fire and you could only save one person, me, Mom, or Dad, who would you choose?" Irma asks.

"Don't know."

"Come on, just say."

"You, I guess."

"Grandma or me?"

"You."

"Samuel or me?"

Vilda stops dead on the stairs and turns around. "What did you say?"

"Would you save me or Samuel if there was a fire?"

"Why would I save Samuel?"

A hundred horses are galloping through her chest. It feels like Irma knows something she shouldn't, as though she's opened a door into Vilda's head and peered inside. Can she tell from looking at her face? Into her eyes? Or did she see his name on her phone?

After a long pause, Irma shrugs and says: "Don't know. I just said a random name." They resume climbing the stairs. Irma's breath on her back.

"What about you?" Vilda says. "Who would you save out of me, Mom, and Dad?"

"You," Irma replies. "If I could only save one person in the entire world, I'd save you."

31

THE LILACS CAST bluish green shadows across the lawn. Vilda sits down where they're darkest. The phone in her hand feels like a wrapped gift, tied with shimmering ribbon.

She knows Samuel has replied, because she glimpsed his name on the screen, but she doesn't know what the reply says. Hasn't had the courage to read it yet, hasn't wanted to, has wanted to save his words until the right moment.

The screen is dark and shiny. To think, all the things it contains. Everything. She both wants to read and doesn't, tingly with fluttering anticipation.

Eventually, she unlocks the phone. Samuel has sent two messages.

Iv mejdik.

Le gus dån Ábmuda mánájmánná?

It takes her a few seconds to realize she actually understands what Samuel's asking.

But just to be sure, she still opens the dictionary app, double-checking the last word. Yes, she was right, she understood the whole question without help: *Are you Ábmut's grandchild?*

Finally, he's figured out who she is.

Lev, she replies.

After sending the message, she realizes she should have written more. Asked him something back, said something to keep him engaged.

And suddenly, it doesn't feel as difficult anymore.

They write about all kinds of things, things Vilda has never talked to a guy about before. Like, what they're up to this summer and what TV shows they're watching. It's slow, she keeps the dictionary open in the background, but the important thing is that it's happening. The harder Samuel's messages become to interpret, the more powerful the rush when Vilda understands them—and when she manages to compose a reply. She can't be sure the spelling and grammar come out right, but Samuel seems to understand what she's writing, at least. That in itself is so wild she has to just stare into space for a bit every once in a while. She's having a conversation in Sámi, imagine that. And with Samuel.

When Samuel asks what kind of music she listens to, she panics and opens his Spotify profile. Writes the names of his most played artists, even though she's never listened to them herself.

Kanye West, 2Pac, stuff like that. But right now it's mostly Ant Wan.

She has a reply within seconds. *Are you serious?*

Yes. What, you don't like them?

I do, they're some of my favorites. I was just impressed.

Nothing in the world can stop the smile spreading across Vilda's face. This is just incredible.

Eventually, Samuel says he has to go.

Vuojnnalin, Vilda writes. Just like Áddjá told her the last time they saw each other.

See you.

Samuel likes her message. A small, red heart appears in the corner of the bubble. A *heart*. She's so overwhelmingly ecstatic she has to lie down in the grass. She stares up at the sky, watching the clouds slowly drift by high above her. She wonders if Áddjá's up there. If he can see her now. Maybe he's proud. She hopes he can see how big she's smiling down here on earth.

Then something lands ever so lightly on her thigh. She pushes herself up onto her elbows to see what it is. It's a white butterfly, which makes her think about the funeral. What if it's the same butterfly as the one she saw on the way to the car? No, it can't be, but it looks a lot like it. It just sits there on her leg for a good long while without flying off. When she gingerly reaches out, it crawls onto her finger.

Just as she's beginning to wonder if it's injured, it suddenly whirls back up into the sky.

Irma's playing Nintendo Switch on the sofa when Vilda comes bouncing up the stairs. She calls out something Vilda doesn't catch, but Vilda really can't be bothered to listen to Irma right now. Instead, she hurries to her room, eager to tell someone about the joy she's feeling. She catches herself once again wishing Alma was there, so she could show her what she and Samuel have been writing to each other. Or show Alma him, first of all. She doesn't even know he exists.

Right now, Vilda just wants everything to be normal again. But disappointment and doubt are still lingering. She's not entirely sure Alma really cares about her anymore, genuinely cares. And yet she misses her so much. Vilda isn't used to being away from Alma for this long, physically or mentally.

She picks up her phone again and opens Snapchat. Checks out Alma's latest story. In the picture: an ocean-blue rolling suitcase, a soda bottle, and a pair of feet wearing tennis shoes. From the looks of it, she's at an airport.

Vilda opens the Snapchat camera. Takes a selfie, choosing a filter that makes her eyes bigger and her cheeks pink. Across the picture, she writes: *Are you on your way home?*

She hesitates. Is it weird to write now, after barely being in touch at all while Alma was gone? Maybe not, Alma has snapped from time to time, after all. Although Vilda hasn't replied much. She hits Send.

Then she takes her diary out of her nightstand. Sits down at her desk and writes out the whole conversation she had with Samuel. Drawing hearts all around it, coloring them in with a red felt-tip pen. On the next page, she draws the butterfly from memory, the way it perched on her finger, not moving. Because it was white, she has to fill the world around it with color to make it visible.

Her screen lights up. It's Alma, replying.

Yeees, she writes. *We have to hang soon, I miss you!!*

32

ABOVE THEM, CLOUDS drift like cotton candy across the turquoise sky. Birds are singing among the pines and birches. The lake is sparkling, and children are playing and splashing in the water. It feels like the sun is right, right next to her skin.

Vilda hears Alma turn over on her towel. Feels her eyes on her but doesn't know how to respond. She closes her eyes behind her sunglasses.

"Hey," Alma says. "How have you been?"

"I'm doing better now."

She's not actually entirely sure that's true. She should be doing better now, but it doesn't quite feel like she is. Sometimes she forgets everything that has happened for a minute, but the second she thinks of Áddjá, her feelings eat her up from inside, again and again and again.

When she looks at Alma, it feels weird to see her, somehow. It's weird that she's here now, after everything. The hurt comes back every time Vilda reminds herself of the flippant reply Alma sent after reading her long Snapchat message. Why didn't she say more? Didn't she care that Áddjá had just died?

Vilda's hoping Alma will mention it now but is disappointed again when she instead changes the subject and starts telling Vilda about a guy who was staying at the same hotel as her family. His name's Ulrik; he's fifteen and Norwegian. One night, when they went out to the pool together, she put her hand behind his head and kissed him. She'd intended to say something first, but it was as though there were no words. And Ulrik had felt the same way.

She shows her a picture. Vilda shades the screen with her hand. Ulrik's as tanned as Alma, with a tangle of blond curls hanging in front of his eyes. A few freckles sprinkle his nose and cheeks.

"He's cute," Vilda says, giving Alma her phone back.

"Cute? He's so fit I think I might die and be resurrected like Jesus at Easter."

Vilda has to smile. Alma really is back. "You're insane."

"Sure, but come on! His eyelashes are the nails nailing me to the cross."

Alma spreads her arms and legs in the sand. Tilts her head to the side, letting her tongue dangle out of her mouth.

"Then I suppose I'll have to inform Ulrik that you've unfortunately passed away and can no longer be his lady love."

Alma gives a jerk, as though she's been startled awake. Waves away a stubborn horsefly buzzing around her head.

"Didn't you hear the part about my resurrection? Besides, we have a date tonight."

"I thought he lived in Norway?"

"He does, but, like, on Zoom," Alma replies. "We're going to watch a film together. There's this website that lets you do that."

A bird lands in the sand next to them, pecking at the fudge wrappers next to Alma's towel. Vilda sits up, taking a sip of her pear juice. She swats at a mosquito trying to settle on her ankle.

"So, found anyone good-looking here in Jokkmokk?" The moment the words are out, Alma claps a hand to her mouth. "Oh my god, I'm so sorry. As if you'd be thinking about guys when your grandpa just died."

Vilda hesitates with Samuel's name on the tip of her tongue. She screws the lid back on the bottle, running her fingernail across its ridges. Telling Alma suddenly feels really hard. She doesn't know how to make Alma understand her grief. That it's taken over everything, but that at the same time, in a way, life goes on.

"I've actually been texting with a guy."

Alma's eyes widen. She heaves herself up into a sitting position. "Wait, seriously? Who?"

"His name's Samuel."

"Samuel, who? How old is he? Is he Sámi? What have you been talking about?"

Vilda laughs, grinding her bottle into the sand. "He's Sámi. And he speaks Sámi. I've actually started to teach myself."

Alma nods slowly. She actually looks impressed.

"All right, wow," she says. "So the two of you can get together and make babies and speak Sámi to them. That's adorable. Imagine how proud your áddjá would be if he knew."

Warmth wraps itself around Vilda like a soft blanket. It feels good to hear Alma talk about Áddjá like that—maybe she does understand a little, after all. Vilda rests in that thought, watching two little kids dipping their chubby legs in the lake. They laugh and shriek as though it's the most fun thing they've ever done.

Alma rips open a bag of chips. They crunch between her teeth as she chews. "So, what did you talk about?"

"All kinds of stuff. He said he was impressed by my music taste, among other things."

"*God*, seriously! Let me see!"

Vilda opens the conversation and hands the phone to Alma. Her eyebrows shoot up, then her face turns solemn.

"I understand, like, none of this, apart from the artists' names. But that's not the kind of music you listen to, is it?"

"It is, actually. I started getting into it while you were away."

"Fine," Alma says, handing the phone back. "Look, if he said he was impressed, that's a good sign. I think he likes you."

"You do?"

Alma waves her hands in front of her face. "They call me a guy expert for a reason."

Birds are singing inside Vilda now. What if Alma's right and Samuel really does like her? They did text for quite a while.

Vilda and Alma go swimming in the lake. Alma shrieks, yelling that the water in Cyprus was a hundred thousand degrees warmer than here. Goose bumps cover her tan skin. Vilda dives under. It feels like her head's going to crack from the cold until she gets used to it. The deeper she goes, the better it feels. Before long, all the pain is gone.

Evening has come by the time they're done swimming. Alma holds a towel up around Vilda so she can get changed. Mosquitoes swarm around her when she pulls off her wet bikini and drops it in the sand. She pulls on clean underwear, shorts, and a T-shirt.

"Vilda! Alma!"

This time, she recognizes Erica's voice straight away. Siri's walking next to her, and behind them is the rest of the A-Traktor posse: Johannes, Lucas, and some other people from school.

Erica throws her arms around Alma's neck, squeezing her hard. "I haven't seen you in ages. How was your trip?"

That's all the encouragement Alma needs to launch straight back into the story of Ulrik. Vilda glances over at Johannes from time to time, thinking about the comment he left on Instagram. He never reacted to her reply and for some reason, that makes her nervous.

What did he think when he read it? He doesn't even seem to notice Vilda now.

"So, the funniest thing happened at football practice today," he says, loudly enough to cut Alma off. "We were playing a practice game, right, and then Hasse just yelled out: *You have to go deep boys. Come on, penetrate!*"

"That's fucking hilarious," Lucas says.

Apparently, Vilda's the only one who doesn't find it funny. She chuckles a little through her nose while everyone else howls with laughter. It's very warm, even though it's getting late—sweat covers her face, her palms, the back of her knees.

A group of older guys has gathered farther down the beach. Smoke billows around them—even at that distance, Vilda can smell the cigarettes. The music blaring from their speakers makes the ground shake. The bass line finds its way into her body, forcing her heart to beat in time.

Suddenly, she notices Johannes looking at her. He fixes her firmly.

"Hey, by the way," he says. "You looked hot in that gábdde."

Everyone stops talking. Erica frowns. The only sound now is the music the older guys are playing. Vilda can't tell if Johannes is joking or not—he looks serious. Only Lucas snickers a little on the sidelines.

"Thanks," she replies neutrally. Then she waits for the other shoe to drop.

"I mean, you looked properly Sámi. Even though everyone knows you're not."

She's so unprepared for his comment, she's lost for words. Her heart pounds harder in her chest, as though her body's preparing to go to war. She glances over at Siri, wants to know if she agrees, but she's staring at the ground.

"What are you talking about?" Alma says. "Of course she's Sámi."

Erica has taken a step closer to Johannes, her eyes are darting in his direction. He pays no attention to her.

"But Vilda," Erica says, her eyes still on Johannes, "you didn't exactly have a good explanation for why you didn't go to the Sámi school when I asked you about it."

Inside her: a small flame sparks to life. She's been sad for so many days, she's been insecure, but this is something else. A new, unfamiliar feeling.

"It wasn't my choice where I went to school," Vilda says, doing her best to keep her voice steady. "I told you that, Erica. And besides, you don't have to go to Sámi school to be Sámi. Is that so hard for you to understand?"

She surprises herself by saying all of that. Before the summer, she would never have stood up for herself if someone had laid into her like this.

"Then why don't you have a Sámi surname?" Lucas pipes up. "You don't even speak Sámi, do you?"

"Of course she does," Alma says. She has moved so close to Vilda their arms are touching. "You do, right, Vilda? You've been learning."

Johannes sneers. "I'll believe that when I hear it."

Vilda hides from Johannes's eyes, looking up and down the beach while she tries to think of something to say. She lets her eyes linger on the group of older guys and their smoke. One of them turns a can upside down over his mouth, and that's when she spots him—Samuel. He's laughing loudly at something his friend's telling him. Vilda can see all the way from where she's standing that his eyes are glowing.

She nudges Alma with her elbow. Speaks quietly right next to her ear so the others can't overhear. "Samuel's here."

"What?"

"With those guys over there."

Alma turns to look. "Seriously?"

"What the fuck are you staring at?" Johannes says. He's looking at the guys now, too. "Are they your older brothers or something?"

Alma pulls her hair forward over her shoulder. Fiddles with the tips of it. "Vilda's been texting with one of those guys," she blurts out. "In Sámi."

Panic. Why on earth would she tell them that? Vilda shoots Alma a look of despair.

"So she definitely speaks Sámi, I mean. Whatever *you* might think."

For the first time since they got there, Siri looks up at Vilda. She actually looks curious. Johannes laughs, but it sounds more like a snort. Everyone else in his posse is quiet now, watching the scene playing out in front of them.

"So go over there, then," he says. "Let's hear it."

Her body tenses involuntarily: her legs, her bottom, her stomach. Her hands and jaw. "Yeah, right."

"That's what I thought: you don't know how."

Alma nudges Vilda. "Come on, you do know Sámi. I've seen it."

"Sure, but . . ."

"You can do it!" Alma's lips are right next to Vilda's ear. She whispers: "Besides, it seems like Samuel really likes you. It might make him happy if you go over and say hi."

Alma's breath is a warm comfort against Vilda's cheek. Vilda wants to wrap it around herself, bring it with her. Then, suddenly, he appears to her again—Áddjá. As a feeling more than a thought. What if he could see her now. Would he be proud of her, like Alma said?

Hold on, what if he *does* see her? What if he's watching her right at this moment? She can't let him down.

Vilda looks back over at the guys. Fiddles with the hem of her shirt, pressing the fabric in under her fingernails. She hates Johannes and his stupid challenge, but maybe it could lead to something good? At the end of the day, she really does want to be with Samuel, and they had fun texting. The next step should be to talk to him outside of Instagram. Who knows when she'll bump into him again?

But it's not as easy as she wishes it was. Just like at the pool, it's as though her body's freezing up. Her feet have sunk into the sand, and her muscles are refusing to move.

"Can you come with me?" she whispers, her nose almost touching Alma's cheek.

Alma looks like she's considering that for a second, then she suddenly screams so loudly it hurts. "Oh my god, nooooo. I completely forgot about my film date!"

She pulls her phone out of her pocket and makes a frustrated noise when she sees what time it is.

"I really have to go. Ulrik must be wondering where I am." She folds up their towels and shoves them in her backpack, throws Vilda's empty bottle in after them. "Are you coming, Vilda?"

Relief makes Vilda's tense muscles relax; suddenly it's easier to breathe. She's just about to pick her bikini up from the ground when she notices Erica rolling her eyes. Erica leans closer to Johannes, putting a hand in front of her mouth, as though she were whispering, but still speaks loudly enough for Vilda to hear.

"She probably doesn't even know that guy. Super convenient that they have to leave right now, if you know what I mean."

And just like that, Vilda doesn't want to leave anymore. This is her chance, the chance she's been waiting for. To go up and talk to Samuel and at the same time prove to Johannes and his stupid friends that she does speak Sámi should be like killing two birds with one stone.

"You go," she says to Alma. "I'm staying."

"Are you sure?" Alma sounds unsure. "I think Ulrik will be disappointed if I stand him up."

"Probably."

She smiles uncertainly. "All right, but call me after, okay? You can do this."

Vilda nods. She shoots Johannes a withering look, then she walks away, but not in the same direction as Alma. Forcing her legs to keep moving takes everything she has. The sand is electric, sending shocks through her toes, feet, up her legs. The lake laps gently against the sand next to her, little waves following her footsteps, curious about what's going to happen next.

She walks straight over to the group of guys.

One of them looks up when she approaches; she recognizes him from the pool. He gives the guy sitting next to him a shove. They don't take their eyes off her. But Vilda's not interested in them; she cares only about Samuel.

"What's up," the first guy calls out.

The music fades and suddenly everyone's looking at her. Their eyes make her legs tremble. Her stomach flips, as though she were on a merry-go-round or a roller coaster.

Free falling.

"Buoris, Samuel," she says. Her whole body's sizzling and crackling now. She glances back at Johannes and his posse, their curious eyes. She frantically searches her brain for something else to say, and in the end, she just goes for it.

"Man suohtas duv iejvvit."

"Buoris." He looks up at her, a quick smile. Then he looks down, away. Is that it? If you tell someone it's nice to meet him, can't he reasonably be expected to say more than just hi back?

She fumbles for more words.

"Mejt dån . . ." The other guys start snickering, distracting her. She shakes her head—it takes a lot of effort to put together sentences. "Gåk dån vieso?"

Samuel stares at the ground, rubbing his hands together. Why isn't he saying anything? The silence is unbearable. She waits and waits for him to look up at her again, for him to say something, but he doesn't. She can tell from looking at his face that his jaw's clenched.

The guys look from her to Samuel and back again. One of them grins. "Can't you hear your girlfriend talking to you, Sam?"

Another one chimes in: "You've moved down the age brackets since last time, I see. This one might be a bit on the young side though, don't you think?"

"Come off it," Samuel replies. A line between his eyebrows. "She's obviously not my girlfriend."

His words are a slap in the face, her skin reddens from the impact. A few of the guys laugh. They look like dogs, their long tongues lolling. Samuel shakes his head at his friend, who's jeeringly poking him.

"Is that really what you think of me?" he says.

Vilda doesn't know what to do with her legs, her arms, her hands. They hang down her sides, trembling. She looks back over her shoulder, but it's hard to tell if Johannes and the others can hear what Samuel's saying.

Then she spots her wet bikini in the sand. It's too far away for them to see the strawberry print.

She doesn't have the courage to look at Samuel anymore, so she studies the discarded cans in the sand, the shoes, the rocks.

Her body's struggling to get enough air. Her feet have grown roots again; she can't move. Mosquitoes swirl around her, but she no longer has the strength to fight them.

"How long is she going to stand there?" one of the guys asks.

"It's your girlfriend, Sam," another says. "You talk to her."

"How many times do I have to tell you I don't date little kids?"

She flinches. Suddenly, her feet break free of the ground, her body unfreezes, and the soles of her shoes catch fire. She runs away. Sprints past Johannes, Erica, Siri, and the others. She has time to see that Johannes is laughing and Erica's eyes are sparkling as she stares adoringly at him. The sight makes Vilda run even faster, run as fast as she can until she can't hear the voices behind her.

She doesn't realize she left her bikini at the beach until she tumbles through the front door. She kicks off her sandals, slinking into the bathroom without saying hi to Mom or Dad. Brushes her teeth with a shaky hand. The face she sees in the mirror is bright red and warm. She doesn't even want to know what she must have looked like on the beach, in front of all those people.

When she gets to her bedroom, she takes off her clothes to change into her nightgown. Just as she is about to throw her shorts onto the desk chair, she freezes. Has to swallow and swallow again to hold back the tears.

A stain has spread across the crotch, dark and blood-red.

33

PAIN CRASHES OVER her like a wave. Sinking its teeth into her body, boring into her, refusing to let go. It hurts so bad that Vilda can't think or breathe. She throws up into the plastic bowl they use for their Friday night chips.

The pain forces her into bed. The ceiling looks blurred above her. When she shuts her eyes, a tear trickles down her cheek. She wipes it away, setting her jaw.

All day she lies there. Mom washes the bowl and brings salty crackers and a glass of strawberry squash. Runs her cool hand over Vilda's forehead.

"Sweetheart, you're as white as a sheet. I wonder if it's something you ate?"

Vilda can't think what that would be, but it feels like a shark is mauling her insides. The pain stabs and throbs in the lower half of her stomach. She puts a hand there and winces.

"Are you in pain?" Mom asks.

"Yes, my stomach hurts," Vilda replies. "And my back. My whole body, actually."

"Your uterus?"

"Uh, what?"

"Oh, sweetie," Mom says. "I can't believe that wasn't my first thought. You're having your period, aren't you?"

Vilda shoots her a look. "Seriously, you saw me throw up, right? This isn't exactly period cramps."

Mom gives her a smile full of pity. "The women in our family have difficult periods. It was like that for both Áhkko and me, and maybe you, too."

"But I didn't feel anything last time."

Mom shakes her head. "It can be different right at first, before everything gets going properly."

Vilda is given both acetaminophen and ibuprofen, a wheat cushion on her stomach, and a heating pad underneath her back. Mom tucks her in, closes the curtains, and turns on Vilda's string of heart-shaped fairy lights. Then she sits down on the edge of the bed and says, "Hey?"

"What?"

"I've been thinking we should go through Áddjá's things soon. Decide what we want to keep and what we're going to sell or donate. But it can wait until you're feeling a bit better."

Like that's ever going to happen. No, Vilda knows she's never going to feel better, that she's never going to be ready to clean out Áddjá's house. Never, ever. She'd rather throw up every day for the rest of her life.

Mom strokes Vilda's leg through the duvet.

"I know it's hard," she says. "It's not easy being a teenager, and it's certainly not made any easier by losing a loved one."

What do you say to something like that? Vilda just shakes her head.

"Angel. I'm going to let you rest now, but shout if you need anything."

There are so many things Vilda needs, but she knows Mom can't give her any of them. She can't do anything about what happened at the beach, or the pain, or the grief.

"Oh, by the way," Vilda says when Mom's almost out the door. "I lost my bikini."

"Lost? Have you looked everywhere?"

"Mm. I think I left it at the lake."

"We'll have to go see if it's still there, then. And if we don't find it, we'll get you a new one when you're feeling better," Mom says before closing the door behind her.

Silence descends once she's left. Vilda lies there, alone. Feeling like a warm, disgusting puddle. She wants to close her eyes and disappear, but every time she does, she's back at the beach, surrounded by the scornful eyes of the guys. She remembers their dog tongues lolling as they laughed at her. Samuel's words hurt almost more now, looking back.

She's obviously not my girlfriend.

How many times do I have to tell you I don't date little kids?

She forces the memory down, shoving cracker after cracker into her mouth. Sucking on the salty mass. It sticks behind her teeth, to the roof of her mouth; her whole being feels soft and soggy. The squash isn't cold anymore. And it doesn't really taste like strawberry, either, come to think of it. Strawberries taste nothing like this.

Eventually, her brain manages to put some distance between itself and the pain. Vilda takes the opportunity to breathe. Sucks in as much air as she can through her nostrils. She tries to close her eyes without thinking, but there's no controlling her mind.

While she sleeps, she dreams about being eaten by black dogs. Once there's nothing left of her, they lap up the blood on the ground, licking their lips with dark red tongues.

34

VILDA WAKES UP to a damp sheet. When she rolls onto her side, there's a sudden gush between her legs. She gets up, throwing the duvet aside so she can see the sheet.

It looks like someone's been killed in her bed. Brutally stabbed to death.

She hurries into the bathroom and pulls off her panties. The blood has flooded her pad, soaking the fabric. Vilda just can't take it anymore. The underpants end up in the garbage, pad still attached. Then she gets into the shower and scrubs away the blood on her thighs.

She turns the temperature down until the jet pummeling her skin is ice cold. So cold it hurts. In the end, it hurts so bad the pain in her stomach and heart subsides a little.

When she gets back to her room, someone has already removed the bloody sheet.

There's just a faint stain on the white mattress.

Dad knocks on the doorjamb, holding up a folded sheet. The shiny, rustling, fitted one. Vilda shakes her head when he holds it out to her.

"Not that one."

"What's wrong with this sheet?"

"It just sucks, get another one. A white one, without the elastic. Where's Mom?"

"She took Irma to the stable. And if this sheet isn't up to your standards, you'll have to go get another one yourself."

Vilda clenches her jaw. Swallowing and swallowing the tears in her throat, digging her nails into her palms. Mom would never have been like this. She would have known which sheet to get.

"But why? Why can't you get me one?"

"I did. You know where to find them."

"Just grab me another one."

"This is the one I brought."

Dad holds out the folded sheet again. Eyebrows raised. She snatches it from him and hurls it at the window so hard the blinds clatter against the glass.

"Then I'll sleep without a sheet. I hope I get blood all over the damn mattress."

Dad's face goes dark, and suddenly there's a warning finger in Vilda's face. She doesn't flinch. Dad's jaw is set, his lips thinner than usual. His eyes are hard and stern.

"Watch it," he says. "That's not how you speak to your parents."

Vilda raises her hand until it's front of Dad's face, gives him the finger until he backs away. He lets out a string of curses on his way out the door.

SKETCHING THE NIGHTMARE dogs, she pushes down so hard the charcoal breaks. She smears the blackness across the paper, coloring the blood red. Turns to a new page, a quick sketch of Samuel. His entire face is black. Darkness streams down from the top of his head, dribbling down his chin.

She deletes all screenshots of him from her phone. Unfollows him on Instagram. Rips out page after page from her diary, crossing out his name with black marker. The ink seeps through the paper, staining her fingers. Vilda scrubs hard with soap, but she can't get the black off.

Thinking about the evening at the beach is unbearable. The shame makes her lungs contract, makes her burst into tears at the dinner table. Mom strokes Vilda's hair, says, *Sweetheart, my little sweetheart.* As if, somehow, she does understand how Vilda feels after all.

How could Vilda make such an idiot of herself, not just in front of Samuel, but in front of everyone else, too? And how could they be so mean? Johannes and Lucas have never been particularly nice. But Erica? What kind of friend is she when she sides with Johannes and keeps questioning Vilda, again and again? Rage simmers steadily beneath all her other feelings. Why is she friends with people who treat her that way? How has she not seen it before? The only one who actually stood up for her, who didn't stay quiet or agree with Johannes, was Alma.

Alma has texted several times, asking how it went, but it feels too big to text about; it hurts too much. Vilda knows she should explain what happened, but she's worried Alma won't understand how devastated she is—again. So she hasn't written back. Maybe it would be easier to call.

She opens her contacts. Before she can scroll down to Alma's number, her thumb freezes against the screen. The first name on the list is a knife to the chest. Áddjá. Everything's still there: their texts, call history, proof they talked. The times, the dates.

Everything's there, except him. She reads their last texts.

Mån ähtsáv duv.

Ja mån duv, gieres manna.

She bursts into tears again, out of nowhere, a grief so deep she has to press a hand to her mouth. She would do anything to speak Sámi with Áddjá one more time. Anything in the whole world.

She puts her finger on the phone symbol, not really knowing why—she just does it. She can't stop herself. She has to talk to Áddjá, she really has to, or she won't be able to bear it.

But no one answers when she calls.

THE SMELL OF Áddjá still fills the hallway when Mom unlocks the front door. Vilda kicks off her crocs and enters with Irma on her heels. Áddjá's house is so quiet. The only sound is their footsteps across the creaking floor and Mom blowing her nose in the kitchen.

Sniffing and sobbing. Vilda pretends not to hear, leaves Mom be.

Áddjá's house is large. He didn't move after Áhkko died, just lived there by himself for another ten years. He always said she was still there, in the rooms. Vilda never really understood what he meant, but now she reckons he might have been right. There's something in the air in this house, an energy so warm and full of love, even with Áddjá gone. There's no place on earth where Vilda feels as safe.

She tiptoes up the stairs, into the bedroom. The bed catches her when she leans back and falls. The pillow is unused to the shape of her head, was expecting another. If she really tries, she can still feel the warmth of Áddjá in the sheets. They've absorbed his smell, holding on to it for Vilda. She buries her nose in the fabric. The more she sniffs, the fainter it gets. As though the smell is slowly dissipating, even though it was so strong when she first stepped through the door.

Her nose can get used to it. Her heart can't.

Lying in Áddjá's bed, she feels small and round. Like the knot in her stomach, in her throat, that's all she is now. She thinks about what they've come here to do. They're going to sort through Áddjá's things: throw away, sell, or save. Something hard and dark is moving through her body. Is someone else going to have his things now? His furniture, books, house? She doesn't want that. It's her áddjá, hers and Irma's. No one's allowed to take him from them.

She closes her eyes. And all at once, her anxiety fades and her muscles relax. Next to her in bed, right behind her, is Áddjá. He runs his fingers through Vilda's hair, stroking her head. His hand is big and warm. Áddjá doesn't say anything, but that's okay. Vilda can feel his presence in every part of her body.

35

MOM AND IRMA appear in the doorway. "Are you ready, Vilda?"

She isn't, and likely never will be, but she nods anyway. Vilda knows there's no point arguing. It's time. Besides, she wants to see if there's anything of Áddjá's she might be allowed to keep.

"I'm going to run some of the things we find here over to Aunt Aina, so she can have a look, too," Mom says. "Would it be okay if I left you here alone for a bit, later today?"

They nod.

"Good. It's so nice of you to help out."

They start upstairs. Mom has brought moving boxes. She writes on them with a black marker: things to be saved, things to be donated, and things to be thrown away. They go through Áddjá's books, his magazines, the things in his desk. Vilda sets aside any book written in Sámi. It's mostly old picture books, but still. The words in them are humming with energy; she can feel it through the covers.

Vilda and Irma sort through old toys left from when they were little. Pixi books, stuffed animals, and dolls. There's nothing Vilda wants to save. Irma hesitates, putting a stuffed gorilla on her lap, but in the end, she throws it in the donate box.

"I'm going over to Aina-siessá now," Mom says once they've worked their way back to the bedroom. "Why don't you go through the things in here while I'm gone?"

She has put out several boxes of jewelry, presumably Áhkko's, on the bedspread.

The metal gleams and shimmers.

"Take what you want," she says. "But try not to fight over it."

They both nod. Vilda has already spotted several pieces she'd like a closer look at.

Mom strokes her hair, then Irma's. "Be right back."

The moment she leaves the room, Vilda picks up a silver brooch. It gleams and glitters.

"This is probably for the gábdde," she says. "So I'm taking it."

From downstairs comes the sound of Mom closing the front door. The car engine turns over and she reverses out of the driveway.

Irma gives Vilda a look. "What if I want it?"

Vilda frowns. Holds up the brooch to her chest, imagining how beautiful it would look pinned to Áhkko's red sliehppá.

"Why? You don't even have a gábdde."

"Who says I need one?"

"Fine, but why can't you pick something else? Like this."

She holds up a necklace with a small cradle ball. Tiny hoops hang from the pendant. It dangles from her fingers.

"No." Irma shakes her head. "I want the brooch."

"You only want it because I took it first."

There's a storm brewing in Irma's eyes. Thunderclouds roll into her normally bright gaze.

"Why do you always get everything?" she says. "Áhhko's wedding gábdde, Áddjá's books, everything!"

"What? I had no idea you were even interested."

Irma's face is turning red. "You think you're the only one who misses Áddjá? Who would like to have a gábdde? He was my áddjá, too, just as much."

A sudden pressure inside Vilda's rib cage.

"But you haven't said anything! You've barely mentioned Áddjá since he died."

"And you have? You never let anyone talk to you at all, about anything."

Irma snatches the necklace from her and hurls it at the wall. "I want my normal sister back. The big sister who cared about me."

The pressure inside Vilda's chest is mounting; it's so strong now her ribs might crack.

Vilda snorts, laughs with despair.

"What are you talking about? I'm still the same person!"

"No, you're not! Mom thinks you're horrible, too. She told me she doesn't even recognize you."

The words are knives, and Irma's plunging them straight into Vilda's guts and twisting them.

"All you care about is boys and Samuel and all kinds of horrible things. Like that shoebox under your bed."

Vilda swallows thousands upon thousands of words. Rage presses its hands against her skin. Banging and thumping, trying to push its way out, it doesn't want to be trapped inside her anymore.

"What did you say?"

"What, it's true. Reading what you wrote made me *barf*."

Her mouth tastes dark. Like all the worst curse words. "What did you read?"

Irma's pacing up and down, her hands clenched. "Why does no one in the entire world care about what I want?"

"Answer me! What the fuck did you read?"

"What do you think? Your disgusting diary."

A precipice, an abyss, there's nothing left to hold on to. "What the fuck's wrong with you? You're fucking sick. Asshole!"

"Put a lock on it if you don't want people reading it."

Vilda wants to kick Irma in the stomach so hard something breaks. Violence is boiling in her veins, hissing and bubbling.

"I *hate* you!"

"Not as much as I hate you, freak."

"Fuck you, Irma. Are you so stupid you don't get that I don't want to be with you every goddamn second? That I don't want to talk to you every minute of every day. That I have a *life* that you're not part of? You don't have to cling to me like some fucking baby all the time."

Irma sneers, rolling her eyes. "You're one to talk."

"What?"

"*Oh, I hope Samuel wants to be my boyfriend! I want to be with him every day!*"

Vilda pictures it in slow motion: her, grabbing Irma's shirt and hurling her against the wall. Like in an action film, when the victim hits the concrete so hard the wall breaks. And if not the wall, then the person. Something has to break. Something has to break, and it has to hurt.

But when she does grab Irma's shirt, that's not what happens. Vilda's not strong enough—she ends up just tugging at it. But Irma still lets out a scream. Her hand swoops past Vilda's face, her nails scratching her cheek. She hisses, spitting in Vilda's eye. The saliva burns, dribbles down her face. Vilda grabs Irma's arms, twisting them back until they creak.

She roars so loudly the words tear up her throat. "I wish you had died instead of Áddjá!"

And then. Behind them: a bang so loud the floor trembles underneath their feet. She lets go of Irma, whipping around. The door to the walk-in closet is wide open, and inside, a box has fallen off its shelf, landing on the floor.

The shock paralyzes them. Vilda searches for some kind of explanation in Irma's face, but the only thing she can see in her eyes is panic.

For a hundred years, they stand stock-still. Neither one of them makes a sound. They both stare at the box, as though it's about to open up. But it doesn't. Absolutely nothing happens.

Once surprise fades, anger and desperation come flooding back. Vilda can't look at Irma anymore. Her feelings are so overwhelming they force her out of the room and down the stairs. She races outside, slamming the front door so hard the house shakes. The ground rumbles beneath her as she races toward the woods. She flies over roots and rocks, leaping from side to side to avoid crashing into anthills, moving so quickly the mosquitoes don't have time to land on her skin.

Only now does she notice the butterflies. They're swirling around her, paper white against the greens of the forest. She's never seen so many butterflies at once, in one place; they're absolutely everywhere, flying as fast as she's running.

There's a massive rock out in Áddjá's forest, a rock as big as a troll. When Vilda and Irma were younger, they used to pretend the rock was a Stállo, a big, horrible giant crouched there among the trees. They knew that when they least expected, he might stand up and stomp through the forest, making the ground shake and the trees snap under his feet. Vilda wants that to happen now. She wants the Stállo to stand up and crash right into the house.

She pushes her way through branches and undergrowth, putting her hands on the rock. Wedging a foot in a hollow in the stone, she manages to heave herself up. She lands on top of the rock. Pushes up onto her feet, gazing out at the forest. Between the trees, she can just make out Áddjá's house. She wonders what Irma's doing inside.

Fuck Irma. Fuck Samuel. Fuck Áddjá, for leaving Vilda here. There's no one in the whole world who understands her now. Really no one, because Áddjá's dead. Áddjá's dead and Vilda's so filled with rage she screams, at the top of her lungs, so loud the birds change direction midair, the ants scurry back into their hill, and the clouds darken. The sun is dislodged from the sky. Not even the sun can be trusted anymore.

She hears a rustling among the trees, a branch snapping. Someone's standing there, just a few feet from the rock.

"Do you really wish I were dead?"

Vilda looks down at Irma. For a few seconds, there's silence. "How could you read my diary?"

There's a long pause before Irma answers.

"Because I didn't know anything about you anymore. It almost felt like you'd disappeared." She grabs a birch branch, picking the leaves off one at a time. "I thought you'd, like, written all kinds of mean things about me in the diary. But you never even mentioned me. It was all just Áddjá and Samuel."

That hasn't occurred to Vilda. But surely it's her diary to write in whatever she wants? Irma had no right to read it.

"I'm not going to be sisters with someone who reads my diary."

"And I'm not going to be sisters with someone who wishes I were dead."

Vilda sighs. "You want me to feel sorry for you now? I don't, you're a fucking psycho."

"*You're* a fucking psycho for saying things like that to me!"

"But seriously, how do you not get that you can't be going through my private stuff? What if I'd done that to you?"

Irma strews the birch leaves across the ground like confetti. "I'm never going to forgive you," she says.

"And I'm never going to forgive you, either. Never in my life."

"Fine, then I'm not going to talk to you ever again."

"Good, I won't have to put up with you for once."

Vilda sinks into a squat. The rock is hard and uneven underneath her. She stares mutely at Irma. Then she says: "Do you know what's in Áddjá's box?"

"No, what?"

"I don't know, either, but I figured you might have looked in it."

Irma shakes her head. Vilda slips off the rock; it scrapes against her denim shorts. "Come on, then," she says. "Let's open it."

36

THE DOOR TO the closet is still wide open. The box is still where it was when Vilda left the room. They sit on the floor on either side of it.

Vilda runs her fingers across the lid. "What if it's not special?"

"What do you mean?"

"It feels like there should be something special inside, because of what happened."

Irma seems to ponder that for a moment.

"The door must have been open a crack, right? And then I guess we accidentally bumped something when we were fighting. Except, why would the box just randomly fall down?"

Vilda shrugs. The box feels rough under her hands.

"I don't know," she says. "Some things can't be explained."

Irma meets her eyes. "All right, are we opening it?"

So, she opens it. Inside is a sliehppá. It's bright red, with squares of yellow, blue, green, and red along the collar. The dickey is decorated with symbols embroidered with pewter thread. On top is a pale yellow Post-it note. *Irma*, it says.

"But what is this?"

When Irma picks up the sliehppá, they realize there's another one underneath.

Another Post-it note. This one says *Vilda*.

Just then, they hear the front door opening. Irma jumps up, runs over to the stairs, and calls out: "Come look at this, Mom!"

Mom takes so long getting upstairs Vilda thinks she might explode. She runs her fingers over the pewter thread embroidery. Irma can't even hold on to her sliehppá—she leaves it on the floor so she can bounce from one end of the room to the other, hugging a pillow.

Mom appears in the doorway. Her eyes take in Vilda and Irma, the open box on the floor, the sliehpá. Her eyes well up.

"How did you find that box? Did you go in the closet?"

"Are they our sliehpá?" Vilda asks. "Or why are our names on the notes?"

Mom moves the jewelry aside and sits down on the edge of the bed, running her hands over her face. Heaving a long sigh.

"He was going to give them to you on your birthday, Vilda."

"What? Áddjá was? Why didn't you tell us?"

Mom takes a tin bracelet from the jewelry box, fiddles with it. "I figured I should wait until the gábde were done, too."

Irma lets out a giggle, her face beaming with anticipation. "Gábde?"

"Yes," Mom says. "Áddjá really wanted the two of you to have your own gábde, with sliehpá and everything else that goes with it."

"But . . . Who's making them?"

"Anneli, Nils-Johan's wife, made the sliehpá. And now she's working on the gábde."

A bucket of ice cubes, straight into Vilda's stomach. "Samuel's mom?"

Mom nods.

"You were so eager to have a gábdde; it was hard to keep quiet. But we wanted it to be a birthday surprise, so I just played along. And then when . . ." She inhales, looking up at the ceiling. "Then when Dad died, I didn't know what to do. I figured it would make you sad if I told you about it on your birthday. That it would make both of you think of Áddjá and that it would bring everything down."

"It wouldn't have made us sad!" Irma's eyes are welling up now, too. "At least not me."

Vilda nods her head, fingering the collar of her sliehppá. "Me neither. Just happy."

"You're right," Mom says. "I think I was actually the one who found the gábde painful to think about, not you."

"When will they be done?"

"Anneli has all the fabric and materials, but she needs more accurate measurements before she can start sewing. My covert measuring wasn't very exact." Mom smiles, wiping the corner of her eye. "You have no idea how hard it is to measure someone's neck without them noticing! I really hope your sliehpá fit. If they don't, the buttons can be moved around, if they're too tight or too loose."

Irma has picked up the necklace she threw at the wall and is spinning it around her index finger.

"Can she measure us right now?"

Mom chuckles, pulling Irma into her arms. Kissing her temple. Vilda smiles up at them from where she's sitting on the floor.

"They might have set off for the mountains, but if we're lucky, they're still home tonight."

Irma wriggles out of Mom's embrace, picking up her sliehppá from the floor. "I want to try mine on!"

Mom helps them tie the ribbons behind their backs and do up the buttons of the collars. This sliehppá fits Vilda better than Áhkko's. To think, she's going to have her very own gábdde now, a gábdde she can wear whenever she wants. It almost feels surreal. The feeling glitters inside her.

Irma's sliehppá seems to fit, too; it's just a little bit loose around her neck.

"We'll ask Anneli to move the buttons," Mom says. She strokes Irma's back before pulling out her phone. "I'll go downstairs and call her right now."

Vilda and Irma stay in Áddjá's bedroom. They're both still wearing their sliehpá. Vilda peeks into the walk-in closet. Inside, she can make out the gábde lined up on their hangers.

"Irma," she says. "Áhkko had a lot of gábde, not just the one I borrowed. Want to see if any of them fit you, so we can see what your sliehppá looks like underneath?"

Irma nods. She looks different than before. All the hardness and sharp edges are gone, only Vilda's little sister remains. Her eyelids are still pink from crying.

The closet smells stuffy, the floor creaks when they step inside. Vilda and Irma do exactly what Vilda and Áddjá did before; they put all the gábde out on the bed so Irma can try them on. Áhkko was a fairly small woman, so they actually find one that fits. At least sort of. Irma's new sliehppá looks even more beautiful now, through the opening at the front of the gábdde. Vilda smiles, tying a belt with tassels around Irma's waist. She can feel something swelling inside her chest, a fluttering in her heart. Two butterfly wings opening.

They run down the stairs, jumping the last step, landing by the full-length mirror in the hallway. Vilda's hands on Irma's shoulders. They stand there in silence for a moment, taking it all in. Their eyes lock in the mirror.

It looks like something new is swelling inside Irma, too.

37

MOM LOADS THE last box onto the trailer and locks the door to Áddjá's house. Vilda looks at the house, the garden, the forest. She's known these trees since she was little. Known every path, every anthill, known exactly how to get to the best blueberry-picking spots. She knows on which side of the house the sun rises, and where its last rays fall. She knows which steps of the stairs creak the most, how to give the front door an extra push to make sure it latches. She knows all those things. She will always know all those things, even though Áddjá no longer lives there, no matter who buys the house next.

She looks back one more time before getting into the backseat. Irma pulls open the door, climbing in next to her. When Mom starts the car, she shoots them a look, eyebrows raised.

"No one's going to sit up front?"

"Nope," they say in unison.

Mom laughs a little, shaking her head. And even though Vilda's sitting behind her, she can tell from her cheeks she has a huge smile on her face.

38

HER BIKINI WASN'T at the lake, so Vilda and Mom drive into Gällivare to buy a new one. Mom suggests a yellow bikini with purple flowers, which comes complete with a swim skirt. Vilda shakes her head. Instead, she tries on a black bikini with a push-up top. It makes her breasts look a bit bigger, there's a faint shadow between them. She runs her fingers over her new cleavage.

"Does it fit?" Mom asks through the curtain.

"Yes," Vilda replies. Because it actually does. It doesn't swallow her curves. It brings them out.

Vilda puts her clothes back on. Her shirt's still warm. When she steps out of the fitting room, Mom takes the bikini top from her, pinching the padding.

"You can take these out," she says, demonstrating. Vilda nods, but she already knows she doesn't want to. Then she might as well have bought an unlined bikini.

On the drive home, Vilda's phone dings. She's surprised to see that it's a message from Siri. They've never texted before.

Just wanted to say that I saw what a jerk Samuel was to you on the beach. Don't take it personally, you were really brave to go over there even though Johannes was being such a douchebag. Btw, had no idea you speak Sámi. Super cool that you've been learning!

All kinds of thoughts crowd into her head. Does Siri know Samuel? Has he been a jerk to other people, too? But above all: does Siri seriously think it's cool that Vilda has been teaching herself Sámi?

Mom glances over at Vilda. "It always makes me so curious when you're beaming like that. Are you texting with Alma?"

She shakes her head. "No, Siri."

"Siri?"

"Yeah, Siri, in my class. She joined last year, remember?"

Mom nods, her eyes on the road. "Is she Rebecka's daughter?"

"Uh, I think so."

"Then you're related. Distantly, but still."

"What? We are?"

"Absolutely, though I can't say exactly how off the top of my head. Unless I'm misremembering, Rebecka's great-grandmother and my great-grandmother were sisters. Your áhkko always kept track of things like that when she was alive."

Vilda smiles. Then she looks down at the screen, reading Siri's message again. Maybe they could be friends?

Gijtto, she replies. The next time Siri texts, it's in Sámi.

39

MOM AND DAD'S bedroom is the only cool place in the house. Vilda sneaks in there after dinner, sees the outline of Mom resting on top of the bedspread. The blackout curtains make the room so dark Vilda has to wait for her eyes to adjust. All day, she's been blinded by the summer sun.

"Hi, sweetheart," Mom says. She sounds a bit sleepy, in a cozy way. Her voice makes Vilda yawn. She crawls into bed next to Mom, wrapping herself in her arms. Feeling Mom's breath against the back of her neck. A warm sigh.

"I want to apologize," Mom says.

"Huh?" Vilda pushes a strand of Mom's hair out of her eyes. "What for?"

"For not realizing how important all the Sámi things are to you. And to Irma. I always assumed you were happy with what you had."

The darkness almost makes Vilda forget that Mom's there. That she has to say something back. She can't see her, just the outline of the edge of the bed and the curtains. A sliver of light around the window frame.

When Mom continues, her voice is different. Thick and high-pitched at the same time. "I guess I feel guilty," she says. "About all the things I didn't give you."

Vilda turns to face Mom. "You don't have to feel guilty," she whispers.

"I just can't help thinking about what things would be like if I'd tried harder. If I'd learned Sámi when I was young, for you. And if I'd been more active with the reindeer, helping Dad out. Then you wouldn't have to take that fight now."

Vilda didn't realize Mom had noticed her trying to learn Sámi. Has she mentioned it to her? Maybe she just figured it out, without Vilda having to tell her.

When Vilda curls up next to Mom, she can hear her mother's heart beating close to her ear. Thump, thump, thump. The sound opens up something inside her—fear, grief. One day, Mom's heart's going to stop beating. Like Áddjá's, like Áhkko's.

Mom clears her throat, sucking in the tears that are about to burst out. "We're going to have to make a decision soon about what we want to do with Áddjá's earmark."

"What do you mean?"

"Originally, I figured we should probably sell the reindeer, but now that you and Irma are taking an interest, that feels wrong. But it's a big responsibility, so we need to talk it through properly."

Vilda hardly knows what to say. "Can we really do it without Áddjá?"

"I'm honestly not sure how it all works, and we're going to have to ask my family for help. Right now, I just want you to know that it's an option, if you want to keep herding in the future."

Vilda snuggles in closer to Mom. She feels calmer now, somehow, but at the same time, she has so many questions.

"Why didn't Áhkko and Áddjá speak Sámi to you?"

"Well, you know that people in Áhkko and Áddjá's generation weren't allowed to speak Sámi at school. That made a lot of families abandon the language altogether. A lot of parents didn't want to teach their children a language that would be a burden to them, so they decided to speak Swedish with them instead. I think they were trying to shield us from the pain they'd experienced themselves."

Vilda wants to ask why Mom never learned Sámi later in life, but it feels so harsh. She doesn't want to make Mom sad. But even so, she can't help but wonder.

"Didn't you want to learn Sámi later? When you got older?"

Her eyes are used to the dark now. Something happens at the corners of Mom's mouth before she answers.

"Yes," she says. "I took a few courses, but it all came to nothing. I was always too afraid to speak."

She takes a deep breath before continuing. "Besides, speaking Sámi wasn't exactly popular back then. Or being Sámi, for that matter. A lot of people were ashamed of it, unfortunately."

Vilda wants to tell her that the shame is still there, that she feels it, too, but that it's in reverse now. She's ashamed that she *doesn't* speak Sámi. That she's ignorant—robbed of her own language. Even though it's not her fault. Or Mom's, or Áhkko's, or Áddjá's.

"And I know I'm not the only one," Mom says. "A lot of us lost our language. Nils-Johan, for example, didn't speak Sámi with his and Anneli's children for a long time. So now, you young people have to fight to reclaim the language."

It feels like someone has thrown the curtains wide open.

"What!?"

"Huh?"

"I thought Samuel's parents always spoke Sámi with him!"

Vilda's so excited she has to get out of bed to keep the feeling growing inside her under control. It fizzes into her legs, arms, fingers. Mom gives her a searching look before answering.

"No, Anneli doesn't speak Sámi, as far as I know. And Nils-Johan chose to speak Swedish with his children, just like Áhkko and Áddjá. I don't think they started speaking Sámi until Samuel was a teenager. When Nils-Johan became ill, probably. At least that was the first time I heard Samuel speak Sámi."

Vilda paces up and down. Samuel *learned* Sámi? But he speaks so well. And here she's been laboring under the misapprehension that all things Sámi were just given to him. That he and she were from completely different worlds and that she could never have what he has, because he had it for free, from birth. Now, it feels like the world has been turned upside down. Everything suddenly seems within reach: the language, the reindeer, the gábdde. Why wouldn't Vilda be able to do what Samuel's done?

Mom heaves herself into a sitting position, studying Vilda. "I know you and Samuel used to play together when you were little, but I didn't think you were still in touch. Do you know each other well?"

Vilda is unable to hold back her smile; it spreads from one ear to the other. Relief is a window, and it's wide open.

"No," she says. "We definitely don't."

40

ANNELI WRAPS A measuring tape around Vilda's chest and jots down numbers in a notepad. Measures her arms, pen in mouth. All Vilda can think about is that Anneli is Samuel's mom, that they're in Samuel's kitchen, and that Samuel might be somewhere in the house right now. She'd *die* if he saw her here.

"I think we'll make the gábdde slightly bigger than you are," Anneli says. "So you have room to grow."

The fridge is full of photographs held up by brightly colored magnets. Vilda squints at them while Anneli measures. A boy, probably Samuel, sitting in a red plastic tub with a shampoo mohawk. To think that he was that little once. Next to him, a black-and-white photo of a bride and groom Vilda doesn't recognize. Another photo shows two herding dogs playing in the grass.

And that's when she spots him. Áddjá. Staring straight at her from a photo.

"Your áddjá meant a lot to Samuel," Anneli says. She must have noticed what Vilda was staring at. "When Nils-Johan was ill, Ábmut helped me and Samuel with the reindeer. He really was a very special man. So wise, such a good teacher. I don't know what we would have done without him."

"Was Nils-Johan very sick?"

Anneli pushes Vilda's hair aside, measuring across her shoulder. "He had cancer. But it's gone now, thank god."

Cancer. Vilda barely knows what to say. Her thoughts are interrupted by creaking steps upstairs. She flinches, looking up at the ceiling.

"Samuel's home?" she asks.

Anneli laughs and shrugs. "I couldn't tell you the last time Samuel was home." She shakes her head. "I've barely seen him since he became a teenager! I don't even notice him coming and going. And now he's about to head up to the mountains for the earmarking."

Vilda exhales. Only now realizing her body had tensed up.

"You know, sometimes, I almost think the gadniha swapped my son for a troll baby. One moment he's normal, and the next he doesn't care one jot what I or anyone else tells him."

Vilda can't help giggling at that. Anneli pats her on the back.

"But I'm sure you're different. I get the feeling you're a wise young lady, as wise as your grandpa, I have no doubt. One thing's for sure, you're as pretty as a butterfly!"

A shudder runs through Vilda. She looks up at Anneli, trying to gauge if she understands what she just said. Does she know that's what Áddjá always used to tell her? But Anneli just smiles.

"All right," Anneli says, rolling her measuring tape up. "All done!"

Before Vilda leaves, Anneli gives her a warm, gentle hug. The kind of hug you want to stay in. To think that Samuel has a mom who actually likes Vilda, who thinks she's wise and pretty. Why doesn't he?

She pulls on her denim jacket in the hallway and is tying her shoes when the front door opens.

She falls a hundred thousand feet into the ground when Samuel spots her.

"Hi," he says.

Vilda can't bring herself to reply. Instead, she makes the bow extra tight across her shoe.

"Oh, by the way," Samuel says. "I wanted to say something to you."

She slips past him and out the door. Walks over to her bike, which she parked next to the front porch. Behind her, he keeps talking.

"Look, I felt kind of guilty. The other night, on the beach. Because I think maybe you see this differently than I do."

"What do you mean by *this*?"

"I don't know," he says. "But it seemed like you got pretty upset. So I want to be clear that I'm not interested in anything."

There's no part of her body that doesn't hurt. Something is spreading through her stomach—an ache, nausea. She can barely breathe through it.

She refuses to let Samuel see how she really feels. Works hard to keep her voice steady. "Then let me be clear that I'm not, either."

"All right, fine then." He hesitates. "I just don't want you to think I'm a jerk, or whatever."

She flicks up her kickstand. Makes fists around her handlebars.

"But if you didn't want to text, you didn't have to reply to begin with," she says.

"Ábmut meant a lot to me, so I wasn't exactly about to ignore his grandchild."

Her cheeks are on fire; it feels like she might throw up. She stares at the ground, trying to find something to focus on. She listens to the buzzing of a bumblebee, to the birds singing their evening songs.

It's a completely normal summer evening. And yet, it really doesn't feel like it. "What I'm trying to say is that I don't want to be anything more than friends," Samuel says, "Because that would be something else entirely."

She nods her head, unable to keep looking at him. Instead, she gets on her bike and turns out of the driveway. Cycling is heavy, heavier than ever before, but she keeps pedaling. Using every last ounce of her strength to get out of there. When she reaches the crest of the hill, something shifts. The summer wind changes direction, wrapping itself around her back, gently pushing her away from Samuel. Forward, toward all the new things waiting for her.

41

SHE KNOWS WHAT she has to do, and she's going to do it now.

She puts everything she needs out on her desk: Mom's dictionary, the books she found at Áddjá's house, a printout of the list of phrases. Highlighters every color of the rainbow. A notebook she's saved for a special occasion.

She starts with everyday words, sentences people use often. She already knows a lot of the food words, but she writes them down anyway: *tjáhtje, mielkke, lájbbe, bierggo*. She highlights some useful phrases, goes over questions and how to answer them. The more she reads, the more she realizes just how much Sámi she already understands. All the things she's heard Áddjá and other older relatives say but has been too afraid to say herself.

Until today.

Downstairs, Irma's playing Nintendo Switch on the sofa. Vilda walks up to the armrest and bends over so they're facing each other upside down.

"Want to have an evening snack with me?"

Irma squints, pushing Vilda's hair out of her face. "Just have to plant a tree first. Sandwich or yogurt?"

"Sandwich."

As Vilda starts getting out bread and cheese, Dad comes into the kitchen. "Ooh," he says. "I might have a sandwich myself."

"No!"

"Pardon?"

"No, I mean . . ." Vilda casts about for an excuse. "You'll have to eat it somewhere else! We're going to play Animal Crossing in here."

Judging by Dad's facial expression, you might have thought she just told him they're moving to Indonesia.

"Is that right?" he says, eyebrows shooting up.

Vilda mimics his raised eyebrows. They're deep into a who-can-raise-their-eyebrows-the-highest competition when Irma pushes in between them and starts spreading butter on a slice of bread.

"So, where's the Animal Crossing?" Dad asks.

"What?" Irma replies.

"Just leave!" Vilda has to usher Dad out of the kitchen. She can't execute her plan until he's gone and Irma's seated at the table.

She opens the fridge, gathering her courage behind the door. This is it. "Mejt sidá juhkat?"

"Huh?" Irma looks up from the kitchen table. She looks like she's just been addressed by an alien.

"Mejt sidá juhkat?" Vilda says again. She holds up the water pitcher and the milk carton. Tries to keep her voice from shaking. "Sidák tjátjev vaj mielkev?"

A couple of years go by. Then something shifts. She can tell something has come unstuck inside Irma. She softens, her shoulders drop.

"Tjátjev," Irma replies.

To think, that something so hard can be so easy once it's done. Vilda fills a glass with water for Irma.

"Gijtto," Irma says before taking a sip.

Something begins to bubble at the bottom of Vilda's stomach. It comes rushing up and out. Vilda barely understands why. Maybe it's relief. But whatever the reason, she can't hold back her laughter. Irma puts her glass down with a bang, stares at Vilda for a split second, and then they both break down. They giggle and snort, Irma whimpers, has to spit the water back into her glass. They laugh so hard the table creaks, tears run down their cheeks, they can barely breathe. Vilda's stomach begins to cramp.

Once Vilda can speak again, she says: "I think you're right."

Irma clears her throat, wiping her cheeks with kitchen roll. "About what?"

"You don't have to be in love."

"No?"

Vilda shakes her head. "It's enough if you love your sister."

42

WHEN ALMA COMES by Vilda's house, she's carrying a wrapped gift.

"I bought you something in Cyprus," she announces. "A birthday present."

"What? You did?"

Alma nods and hands over the present. "I forgot to bring it when we went to the beach; otherwise I would have given it to you then."

Vilda touches the maroon wrapping paper; it's rough and slightly ridged under her fingers.

"Thank you," she says.

"You're welcome. But why didn't you reply to my texts? You had me worried something bad had happened."

The hallway floor feels cold underneath Vilda's bare feet. She backs up and Alma follows, closing the door behind her.

Vilda lowers her voice so no one else in the house can hear. "It wasn't exactly a storming success."

"When you went to talk to Samuel?"

"Mm. He barely replied when I spoke to him. And then he started going on and on about how I'm *definitely not* his girlfriend. But whatever, I'm over it."

Alma shakes her head. "A guy like that doesn't deserve you."

Vilda smiles.

"Come on," she says. "Let's go upstairs."

When they get to Vilda's room, she takes a seat on the desk chair and Alma sits on the bed. Something about her eyes changes. She looks around the room, shooting Vilda nervous glances.

"What's the matter?"

"Listen . . ." Alma's looking out the window now, as though she's searching for the right words. "Since your áddjá died, I haven't known how to act around you. What to say. Especially when I was away and couldn't be here with you."

Vilda looks down at the gift in her lap. Plays with the ribbon. "Mm."

"Everything just came out wrong, you know, when I replied to your message. Because what do you even say to something like that? I was so completely unprepared, and I've never had anything like this happen before. But I really want you to know that I'm so sorry. I can't even imagine how hard it must be for you."

Alma stands up, walks over to the desk, and wraps her arms around Vilda. Vilda rests her head against her, briefly closing her eyes. She doesn't want Alma to let go. She realizes now that she's been waiting for this hug for weeks.

She's glad Alma finally brought it up. That she's showing that she really does care, and that she knows she handled things wrong.

Because even if she wasn't there when Vilda was at her lowest, she's here now. Vilda hasn't known anyone nearly as long as Alma.

They've been friends almost her entire life.

"I've missed you," she says.

"I've missed you, too, so much."

Alma's quiet for a moment, then she says: "Are you going to open your present now?"

They sit on the bed together. Vilda carefully peels off the tape, unwrapping the stiff paper. Inside is a diary, complete with padlock. She's never seen a book like it before—it's the exact right thickness and the cover has illustrations of butterflies with rose gold details. The padlock matches the pink shade of gold exactly.

"Oh my god, it's beautiful! How did you know I needed a new one?"

Alma shrugs. "I just saw it and thought of you. You usually like stuff like that."

She's not wrong. In fact, Vilda likes the book so much she wants to write in it straight away, immediately, just throw out her old diary and start fresh. No one's going to read this diary except her. Especially not Irma. She's going to write about other things now, too, not Samuel but all the things that are going to happen this autumn when she starts eighth grade. And more important, she's not going to write in Swedish anymore. Every word in this book will be in Sámi.

It feels like this diary is a new chance. As though one story has just ended, and another is about to begin.

43

THE HEADSTONE IS warm under Vilda's hands. She runs her fingers over the inscription, touching every letter in Áddjá's name. Her grief is so vast it takes over everything—a mineshaft straight down into her stomach, an explosion that sets every muscle trembling. She doesn't try to stop it. She has learned to breathe through her feelings. Maybe the only way forward is to accept them, let them unfold, and learn to live with them.

The cemetery's quiet and still. There's almost no one else here, except for an older woman tending a grave a few rows away. She's looking after some sun-yellow roses, watering them with a green watering can. Her boots are the same color.

Vilda realizes now that she'd expected Áddjá to be here. She's not entirely sure why she thought that, or *what* she thought, exactly, but she feels disappointed. Nothing here reminds her of Áddjá. Nothing except the stone bearing his name, a stone that wasn't even here while he was alive.

She sits down with her back to the stone and opens her shoulder bag. Pulls her knees up so she can prop the sketch pad against her thighs. The pencils rattle when she sticks her hand into the case and fishes out her favorite. She opens a picture of Áddjá on her phone and begins to draw.

It doesn't come out well. She can't figure out what the problem is, where she went wrong. The contours are right, but something about his expression isn't. It doesn't look like him.

She turns to a blank page.

This time, she closes her eyes and locks her phone, drawing without looking. She can feel Áddjá now. A wave of warmth and love and light. The feeling flows through her fingers, into her pencil, and down onto the page. She draws quickly, hard and soft; it feels as though the pencil disappears—there's nothing between her and the portrait anymore. They're one, she and the paper, she and the pencil, she and Áddjá.

Time disappears. She has no idea how long she's been sitting there, but when she opens her eyes again, the sun has slipped behind a cloud and the woman with the roses is gone. Vilda's bottom hurts.

When she looks down at the paper, Áddjá's eyes look straight into her heart. Finally, she recognizes him. She carefully tears out the page, folds it up, and wedges it in behind a flowerpot, right next to the headstone.

"Dála l dunji," she whispers.

It doesn't even feel all that difficult. The words come almost naturally now; her tongue is getting used to them. She wants Áddjá to hear, wants everyone to hear; she wants to scream and shout. Shout so loud the whole world hears her.

On her way out, she looks up at the sky and calls out: "Mån åhtsålav duv, áddjá!"